He tilted her chi[...]into his eyes. "Is your name really Jody?"

"Y-yes. Jody Vanessa Ingram." She hated that her voice came out in a breathy whisper.

He smiled. "Well, Jody Vanessa. I think it's time you called me Adam. Don't you?"

His deep voice and cool blue eyes seemed to cast a spell on her. She couldn't think with him this close, could barely even breathe.

"McKenzie...I mean, Adam. What's the plan here? Why did you—"

He tugged the rope, pulling them even closer together. "This is where that trust part comes into play."

He grabbed her around the waist.

She read the truth in his eyes and suddenly realized what he was going to do. The rope. The fact that he'd tied the two of them together. "No. No, no, no. Please. I can't do this. I'm too scared. I can't."

Sympathy filled his gaze. He brushed a featherlight caress down the side of her face. "Then I'll just have to do it for both of us."

Adam yanked her forward. She screamed as they tumbled over the cliff.

SMOKY MOUNTAINS RANGER

LENA DIAZ

HARLEQUIN INTRIGUE®

This book is dedicated to my dear friends and fellow authors
Jan Jackson and Connie Mann. Your constant cheerleading and
friendship is priceless. Jan, thank you for helping me through my
plot tangles on this one. I hope you approve of the final product.

ISBN-13: 978-1-335-60430-9

Smoky Mountains Ranger

Copyright © 2019 by Lena Diaz

Recycling programs
for this product may
not exist in your area.

This edition published by arrangement with Harlequin Books S.A.

For questions and comments about the quality of this book,
please contact us at CustomerService@Harlequin.com.

Printed in U.S.A.

www.Harlequin.com

Lena Diaz was born in Kentucky and has also lived in California, Louisiana and Florida, where she now resides with her husband and two children. Before becoming a romantic suspense author, she was a computer programmer. A Romance Writers of America Golden Heart® Award finalist, she has also won the prestigious Daphne du Maurier Award for Excellence in Mystery/Suspense. To get the latest news about Lena, please visit her website, lenadiaz.com.

Books by Lena Diaz

Harlequin Intrigue

The Mighty McKenzies

Smoky Mountains Ranger

Tennessee SWAT

Mountain Witness
Secret Stalker
Stranded with the Detective
SWAT Standoff

Marshland Justice

Missing in the Glades
Arresting Developments
Deep Cover Detective
Hostage Negotiation

The Marshal's Witness
Explosive Attraction
Undercover Twin
Tennessee Takedown
The Bodyguard

Visit the Author Profile page at Harlequin.com.

CAST OF CHARACTERS

Adam McKenzie—When this law enforcement ranger with the US National Park Service discovers a gunman threatening a woman on a remote Smoky Mountain trail, he risks everything to protect her and find out who's trying to kill her, and why.

Jody Ingram—In pursuit of her dream to work in the prosecutor's office, she's made some powerful enemies. Now she and Adam are racing against time and dodging bullets to find the truth.

Tracy Larson—Jody's lifelong friend has gone missing. Adam and Jody must evade their pursuers and find Tracy before it's too late.

Ron Sinclair—This Tennessee senator could have something to hide, or he may be Adam and Jody's only hope for survival.

Damien—Jody and Adam's nemesis rallies his thugs against them. But is he the one calling the shots?

Sam Campbell—Owner of Campbell Investigations, his sudden disappearance raises all kinds of questions. Is he a victim? Or is he part of the conspiracy against Jody and Adam?

Peter Ingram—After Jody's biological parents were killed, Peter Ingram became her foster father. Why did she cut her out of his life years ago?

Chapter One

Adam ducked behind a massive, uprooted tree, the tangle of dead roots and blackened branches his only cover on this wildfire-blighted section of the Great Smoky Mountains. Had the man holding the pistol seen him? He ticked off the seconds as he slid his left hand to the Glock 22 holstered at his waist. When half a minute passed without sounds of pursuit, he inched over to peer up the trail and moved his hand to the radio strapped to his belt. After switching to the emergency channel, he pressed the button on his shoulder mic.

"This is Ranger McKenzie on the Sugarland Mountain Trail." He kept his voice low, just above a whisper. "There's a yahoo with a gun up here, about a quarter mile northwest of the intersection with the Appalachian Trail. Requesting backup. Over."

Nothing but silence met his request. He tilted the radio to see the small screen. After verifying the frequency and noting the battery was fully charged, he pressed the mic again.

"Ranger McKenzie requesting backup. Over." Again he waited. Again, the radio was silent. Cell phone coverage in the Great Smoky Mountains National Park was hit-or-miss. It didn't matter if someone was coming up from the Tennessee side, like Adam, or hiking in from the North Carolina border. Cell phones up here were unreliable. Period. Which was why he and the rest of the staff carried powerful two-way radios that worked everywhere in the park.

With one exception.

The Sugarland Mountain Trail, where the devastating Chimney Tops wildfire had destroyed a communication tower.

Budget cuts meant the rebuilding was slow and had to be prioritized. Rehabilitating habitats, the visitors' center and the more popular, heavily used trails near the park's entrance were high on that list. Putting up a new tower was close to the bottom. So, naturally, the first and only time that Adam had ever encountered someone with a gun in the park, it happened in the middle of the only dead zone.

There would be no backup.

If the guy was just a good old boy out for target practice, the situation wouldn't even warrant a call back to base. Adam could handle it on his own and be on his way. But the stakes were higher today—much higher—because of two things.

One, the faded blue ink tattoos on the gunman's bulging biceps that marked him as an ex-con, which likely meant he couldn't legally possess a firearm and wouldn't welcome a federal officer catching him with one.

Two, the alarmingly pale, obviously terrified young woman on the business end of Tattoo Guy's pistol.

Even from twenty yards away, peering through branches, Adam could tell the gunman had a tenuous grasp on an explosive temper. He gestured wildly with his free hand, his face bright red as he said something in response to whatever the petite redhead had just said.

Her hands were empty and down at her sides. Unless she'd shoved a pistol in the back waistband of her denim shorts, she didn't appear to have a weapon to defend herself. The formfitting white blouse she wore didn't have any pockets. Even if she'd hidden a small gun, like a derringer, in her bra, there was no way she could get it out faster than the gunman could pull the trigger.

Did they know each other? Was this a case of domestic violence? Since the two were arguing, it seemed likely that they *did* know each other. So what had brought them to the brink of violence? And what had brought them to *this* particular trail?

Neither of them was wearing a backpack. Unless they had supplies at a base camp somewhere, that ruled them out as NOBOs on the AT who'd gone seriously off course and gotten lost. Not that he'd expect any northbound through-hikers on the Appalachian Trail in the middle of summer anyway. Most NOBOs started out on the two-thousand-plus-mile hike around March or April so they could reach Mount Katahdin in Maine before blizzards made the AT impassable. But even if they were day hikers, they had no business being on the Sugarland Trail. It was closed, for good reason. The wildfire damage made this area exceedingly dangerous. Now it was dangerous for an entirely different reason.

An idiot with a pistol.

So much for the peaceful workday he'd expected when he'd started his trail inspection earlier this morning.

He switched the worthless radio off, not wanting to risk a sudden burst of static alerting the gunman to his presence. The element of surprise was on his side and he aimed to keep it that way as long as possible, or at least until he came up with a plan.

He belatedly wished he'd dusted off his Kevlar and put it on this morning. But even though he was the law enforcement variety of ranger, as opposed to an informational officer, the kind of dangers he ran into up here didn't typically warrant wearing a bullet-resistant vest. The heat and extra weight tended to outweigh the risks of not having a vest on since the possibility of getting into a gunfight while patrolling half a million acres of mostly uninhabited mountains and forests was close to zero.

Until today.

Still, it wasn't the bullets that concerned him the most. It was the steep drop-off behind the woman. One wrong step and she'd go flying off the mountain. The edge was loose and crumbling in many places, particularly in this section of the trail. The couple—if that's what they were—couldn't have picked a worse spot for their argument.

Sharp boulders and the charred remains of dozens of trees littered the ravine fifty feet below. Branches stuck up like sharp spikes ready to impale anything— or any*one*—unlucky enough to fall on them.

Twenty feet farther north or south on this section of

the Sugarland path would provide a much better chance of survival if the worst happened. The slope wasn't as steep and was carpeted with thick wild grasses. Fledgling scrub brush dotting the mountainside might help break someone's fall if they lost their footing. They'd still be banged up, might twist an ankle or even crack a bone. But that was preferable to plunging into a rocky ravine with no chance of survival.

The gunman and the woman were still arguing. But Adam couldn't figure out what they were saying. Sometimes sounds carried for miles out here. Other times a person could barely hear someone a few yards away. It all depended on the wind and the configuration of mountains, rocks and trees nearby.

At the man's back, a vertical wall of sheer rock went straight up to a higher peak. In front of him was the woman and the sharp drop-off. Sneaking up on him just wasn't going to happen. Either by luck or by design, he'd chosen a spot that was impossible to approach without being seen.

As Adam watched, the man gestured with his pistol for the woman to head south, away from Adam. When she didn't move, he stepped forward. She backed up, moving perilously closer to the edge. Adam drew a sharp breath. If he didn't do something fast, this was going to end in tragedy. He'd have to approach openly, giving up his element of surprise, and hope that cooler heads prevailed.

He unsnapped the safety flap on his holster—just in case—and straightened. Keeping his gaze trained on the ground, he boldly stepped onto the path in plain sight and whistled a tune—AC/DC's "Highway to Hell." It seemed appropriate at the moment.

Continuing to look down and pretending not to notice the couple, his hope was to get as close to them as possible and appear nonthreatening—just a ranger in the mountains, doing his job. Most people didn't realize the difference between informational officers and federal law enforcement rangers anyway. They'd assume the pistol holstered on his belt was for protection against bears or other dangerous wildlife. Usually, it was.

In his peripheral vision, he saw the man shove his pistol into his pants pocket. Adam kept moving forward, head down, increasing the volume of his whistling and tapping his thigh to the beat.

"You gonna run into us or what?" the man's voice snapped.

Adam jerked his head up as if in surprise, stopping a few feet away from the couple. "Sorry, folks. Must have been daydreaming. Pretty morning for it, don't you think?" He smiled and waved toward the mountains around them. "Even with the blight from the wildfires, it's still beautiful up here."

The man watched him with open suspicion as if sizing him up and trying to decide whether Adam really hadn't seen the gun. The woman stared at him, her green eyes big and round behind matching green-framed glasses. But instead of seeming relieved to have help, she appeared to be even more terrified than before.

Adam struggled to maintain his smile. "I'm Ranger Adam McKenzie. You folks lost? Got to admit I'm a bit surprised to see you on this particular trail. Know why?"

Tattoo Guy seemed to come to some kind of decision and offered his own smile that didn't quite reach his dark eyes. "Afraid I don't. Why?"

"Because the trail is closed, for your safety. It's because of the fires last season. You heard about those? Burned over seventeen thousand acres, ten thousand of them right here in the park. Killed fourteen people, too." He didn't have to fake his wince. The fire had been horrible, tragic. Innocent civilians—including children—had perished in the flames. Families had been destroyed. The community was still struggling to recover as best they could. But nothing could replace the precious lives that were lost.

The man glanced at the woman, his eyes narrowed as if in warning. "Can't say that I've heard about that. I'm not from around here."

"What about you, miss?" Adam grinned again. "Sorry. Where are my manners? I didn't catch your name. I'm Adam McKenzie. And you are?" He held out his hand to shake hers, purposely leaving enough space between them so that she'd have to move away from the edge to take his hand.

She looked at the other man as if for permission, then leaned toward Adam, her hand out. As soon as she grasped his hand, he pumped it up and down in a vigorous shake, pulling her even farther away from the edge.

"Your name, ma'am?"

"I, um… Jody. My name's Jody Ingram." She shook his hand, eyes wide with fear.

"Pleased to meet you." Adam let her go and held his hand out toward the gunman. "And you are?"

The man's nearly black eyes dropped to Adam's out-stretched hand while he clearly debated his response. A handshake required that he use his right hand, his dominant hand, the one that had held the pistol earlier. He'd be giving up precious seconds of reaction time if he decided that Adam was a threat and he needed to draw his gun. Which of course was exactly why Adam wanted to shake his hand.

Adam was left-handed.

And his pistol was holstered just a few inches from where his left hand currently hung down by his side.

Come on, come on. Shake the clueless cop's hand.

An awkward silence stretched out between them as no one moved. Adam pretended not to notice. He kept his hand out, waiting, a goofy grin on his face. From the corner of his eye, Adam saw the woman watching them closely, her gaze sweeping back and forth.

Finally, the man mumbled something beneath his breath that sounded suspiciously like "stupid hillbilly" before gripping Adam's hand.

Adam yanked hard, jerking the man off balance. The man stumbled as Adam grabbed the butt of his gun in the holster. But Tattoo Guy was lightning fast. Even as Adam began to draw his pistol, the other guy was already drawing his and swinging it toward him.

Chapter Two

"Drop your weapon. *Now.*" Adam had both hands wrapped around the butt of his Glock. The bore of his gun was aimed directly at the other man's head.

Tattoo Guy stood statue still, his weapon aimed slightly to Adam's left, frozen in midmotion. But one quick twist and a squeeze of the trigger would blast a hole through Adam's gut. The only question was whether Adam could blow the man's brains out before that happened. Not exactly a competition he wanted to wage, especially with a woman a few feet away who was dangerously close to the kill zone.

The seconds ticked by. They stood frozen. The only sounds were the woman's short gasping breaths as she watched the standoff, apparently too terrified to back away to a safer location—preferably behind a thick, solid tree.

Adam didn't dare say a word to her. He didn't even blink as he kept his gaze glued to his opponent and his finger on the frame of his gun, just millimeters from the trigger. He narrowed his eyes, letting the stranger know that he wasn't kidding, wasn't bluffing and wasn't the head-in-the-clouds idiot he'd pretended to be moments earlier.

Tattoo Guy must have read the truth and determination in Adam's eyes, in his stance. He tossed his gun to the ground.

Adam kept his finger right above the trigger, ready to fire at the slightest provocation. Everything about the man screamed danger, and he wasn't taking any chances. "Turn around."

The man hesitated, his gaze darting past Adam.

The urge to check over his shoulder to see what Tattoo Guy was looking at was almost impossible to resist. Did the man have a partner in crime creeping up on Adam? Or was he trying to trick him, distract him? His shoulder blades itched, expecting a bullet to slam into them any second. But he didn't turn around. He focused on the known threat in front of him and waited.

The man finally did as Adam had ordered and turned to face the wall of rock.

Adam kicked the pistol out of reach. "Down on the ground. Put your hands behind your back."

Again Tattoo Guy hesitated. Adam pulled a pair of handcuffs from one of the leather cases attached to his utility belt. He desperately wanted to check on the woman, make sure she was safe, that no one was sneaking up behind *her*. But he didn't dare. Not until he had this guy secured.

When the man finally put his hands behind his back, Adam holstered his pistol in one smooth motion and dropped down on top of him, jamming his knee against the man's spine to hold him down. The man cursed and tried to buck him off. But Adam used every bit of his six-foot-three-inch bulk to keep the stranger pinned.

He slapped the cuffs on the man's wrists, then sat back, drawing deep breaths as adrenaline pumped through him. A bead of sweat ran down the side of his face in spite of the mild, springlike temps this high up in the mountains. From the moment he'd seen the gunman to the moment he'd cuffed him had probably only been five minutes. But it had felt like an eternity.

He stood and pulled his prisoner up with him. After patting the man down to make sure he wasn't hiding more weapons, he grabbed the man's pistol and popped out the magazine. After ejecting the chambered round and verifying that the weapon was now empty, he pocketed the gun and the magazine. Then he slid the man's wallet out of his back jeans pocket, jumping back when the man jerked around, glowering at him.

"Give that back." The man's tone communicated a deadly, unmistakable threat.

"After I check your ID."

A smug look crossed the man's face, a look Adam understood when he opened the wallet. Tucked inside was a hefty amount of cash: twenties, tens, a few ones— a thousand dollars, easy. A heck of a lot of money for someone wandering through the mountains. But that was it. No driver's license, no credit cards, nothing that could shed any light on his identity.

He forced the man to face the rock wall again and returned the wallet with its cache of money to the man's pocket. "What's your name?"

Silence met his question.

"What were you doing up here on a closed trail with a pistol? Why were you pointing it at Miss Ingram?"

Tattoo Guy turned his head to the side, watching Adam over his shoulder. Still, he said nothing. He just studied Adam intently, his eyes dark and cold, like a serpent.

Adam glanced toward the woman, then stiffened. During the altercation between him and the gunman, instead of moving down the trail or ducking for cover behind a tree, she'd backed up close to the edge again.

"Miss Ingram." He kept his voice low and soothing so he wouldn't startle her. "Jody, right?"

She swallowed, then nodded.

"Jody, I'd feel a whole lot better if you'd step away from that sharp drop-off."

She glanced over her shoulder. A visible shudder ran through her as she hurried forward and to the side. She'd been mere inches from falling off the cliff and was exceedingly lucky the unstable edge hadn't given way.

"How about you move over there?" He directed her closer to the wall of rock, a little farther up the path and out of reach of his prisoner if the man decided to launch himself at either of them.

She did as he'd directed. But instead of looking relieved that she no longer had a pistol pointing at her, she seemed even more anxious than before. Her face was chalk white, making her green eyes and matching glasses stand out in stark contrast. Even her lips had lost their color, and her whole body was shaking.

Why?

"Everything's okay now," he reassured her. "You're safe. What's this guy's name?"

She exchanged an uneasy glance with the handcuffed man, then shook her head. "I…I don't know. We, ah, ran into each other on the trail."

Adam glanced back and forth between them, beginning to wonder whether he should put her in handcuffs, too. They were hiding something. What was going on here?

"You're strangers? You've never met before?"

She swallowed. "We've never met. I'd just rounded the curve and he was…there. I…ah…startled him, which is why he drew his gun." She gave a nervous laugh. "I guess he thought I was a bear." Again, she gave a nervous laugh that was anything but convincing.

A smile creased Tattoo Guy's lips as he watched the exchange over his shoulder.

"You don't know each other's names?" Adam asked, giving her another chance to answer him truthfully.

"No."

He shook his head, not even trying to hide his disbelief. "You have a habit of getting into heated arguments with strangers?"

Her face flushed guiltily. "He drew a gun on me. I wasn't happy about that. Things did get a bit…heated… with him demanding to know why I'd snuck up on him. Which, of course, I hadn't. But looking back, I can see how it appeared that way to him." She wouldn't meet his gaze. Subterfuge obviously didn't come naturally to her. So why was she covering for this guy? Or was she covering for both of them?

He tried again, working hard to inject patience into

his tone. "You were arguing with each other over him putting the gun down?"

She cleared her throat. "Yes, pretty much." Another nervous laugh.

Her story had more holes in it than a white-tailed fawn had spots. Instead of rescuing her from a domestic dispute between a couple, had he interrupted a disagreement between a couple of criminals? Were they out here doing something illegal and they'd turned on each other? Or maybe whatever they'd planned was still to come, something far worse than trespassing on a closed trail or carrying a gun into a national park. Adam backed up the path several feet so he could keep Jody—if that was her real name—in his line of sight at a safer distance, just in case she and Tattoo Guy decided to join forces against him.

"Let me guess," he said. "You don't have ID on you, either?"

She cleared her throat again. "Actually, no. I don't. I left my purse in my car, at the trailhead. All I have with me are my keys and my phone."

"Empty your pockets."

Her brow furrowed, and she finally looked at him. "Excuse me?"

"Would you prefer that I pat you down like I did your friend?"

Twin spots of color darkened her cheeks, making her freckles stand out in stark contrast to her pale complexion. Her eyes flashed with anger. "I assure you, he's *not* my friend."

That statement, at least, appeared to be true. But he

could tell she immediately regretted her outburst by the way her teeth tugged at her full lower lip.

His prisoner's eyes narrowed at her, as if in warning. Something was definitely rotten in the state of Denmark, or in this case, the Smoky Mountains. And Adam was determined to get to the bottom of it.

"Your pockets, ma'am?"

Without a word, she pulled her phone out of one pocket, a set of keys out of the other. Clutching them both in one hand, she turned out the lining of her pockets to show they were empty. "That's it. There's nothing else."

"Back pockets, too."

Her mouth tightened but she turned around and turned those pockets inside out.

"All right," Adam conceded. "You can turn around." To perform a complete search, he should pat down her bra. But his years of reading people told him that wasn't necessary. She wasn't carrying.

"Where do you live?"

Again, another look at the handcuffed man as she shoved her keys and phone back into her pockets. "Not far from here. I've got an apartment in town."

"Gatlinburg?"

Again, she hesitated. "Yes."

"Why were you two up here today?"

She chewed her bottom lip.

Tattoo Guy simply stared at him, eyes narrowed with the promise of retribution over Adam's interference in whatever was going on.

"Maybe my question wasn't clear," Adam said. "Why were you both on a closed trail?"

"Closed?" The man sounded shocked. "Really? Miss Ingram, did you see any signs saying the trail was closed?" Laughter was heavy in his voice as he watched her.

"N…no." Her voice was barely above a whisper. "I didn't. I guess I was…enjoying nature too much and wasn't paying attention."

Disgusted with both of them, Adam flipped the radio on again. "Ranger McKenzie to base. Come in. Over." He tried two more times, then gave up.

"I don't know what you two are hiding. But at a minimum you're guilty of criminal trespass. This trail is closed for a reason. The recent wildfires have burned away brush that used to hold the topsoil in place. What the high winds and fire didn't destroy, recent rains did. Entire sections of the trail have been washed away. Trees have been toppled, their roots ripping up most of what was left. The trail is more a memory than a reality anymore. The part we're standing on is one of the best sections left. But it's the exception rather than the rule. You already know that, of course. Because you had to climb over and around some of the damage on your way up. No way you missed it."

He waited for their response and wasn't surprised when neither of them said anything.

"It's also against the law for civilians to carry guns into the park. Care to explain why you had a loaded pistol up here, sir?"

"Protection, of course. I've heard there are all kinds

of dangers in these mountains." He kept his gaze fastened on Jody.

As if she felt his eyes on her, she shivered.

What the heck was going on? Had Tattoo Guy just given the woman a veiled threat? Was *he* one of the dangers he'd just mentioned? Even though Adam had zero doubt that Jody Ingram was covering something, his instincts were telling him that she was a victim here. But since neither of them would talk, he had no choice but to bring both of them in.

"Am I under arrest, *Ranger*?" The man drew out Adam's title into several extra syllables, then chuckled. He wasn't the first to make fun of the ranger title. But Adam wasn't inclined to care. He just wanted this guy off the mountain before he hurt someone.

"For now, you're just being detained, for everyone's safety. We'll sort it all out at headquarters. Those are prison tats on your arms, aren't they? I'm sure your fingerprints are on file. Won't take but a minute to find out who you are once I get you back to base. And if you're a felon with a gun, well, we'll just have to deal with that issue, won't we?"

If looks could kill, Adam would be six feet under right now.

He'd dealt with all types over the years, the worst of the worst back when he'd first started out in law enforcement as a beat cop in some of the rougher parts of Memphis. But because of Adam's own intimidating size, he could count on one hand the number of men who made him uncomfortable. This man was one of them. There was something sinister, jaded, so...empty about him. As if long ago he'd poured out his soul and filled the emptiness with pure evil.

He motioned for him to start down the trail, in the direction toward the Appalachian Trail intersection and Clingmans Dome—a famous lookout point high in the Smoky Mountains. "Take it slow and easy."

His prisoner calmly pushed away from the rock wall. As he started walking down the path, he whistled the same tune that Adam had whistled earlier, "Highway to Hell."

Jody watched him go, fear and trepidation playing a game of tug-of-war across her face. Adam wanted to reassure her. But she'd done nothing but lie to him. Trusting her would be a mistake. Instead, he gestured for her to fall in beside him and they started down the steep incline about ten feet behind his prisoner.

"He can't hear you now." Adam kept his voice low as they carefully stepped around boulders and climbed over downed trees. "What was really going on back there?"

She accepted his hand to help her over a pile of rocks and busted branches. There were pieces of splintered wood and rocks everywhere, making it slow going. The prisoner up ahead navigated the same obstacles with surprising ease for a man with his hands behind him. There was now twelve feet of space between them. Adam frowned and motioned for Jody to speed up.

"Well?" he prodded, watching Tattoo Guy's back.

"I already told you. I didn't see the closed-trail signs and I was walking through the park enjoying the scenery. I rounded a curve and scared that man. He drew his gun. I'm sure he would have put it away, but then you came up and things got…complicated."

"That's how you're going to play this?"

She stared straight ahead.

Frustration curled inside him. "You don't have to be afraid of him. I can protect you, help you find a way out of whatever trouble you're in. Just tell me the truth."

She made a choked sound, then cleared her throat. "I am telling you the truth."

He let out a deep sigh. This was going to be a very long day.

Up ahead, the rock wall made a sharp curve to the left.

"Hold it," Adam called out to Tattoo Guy. "The trail gets much steeper and more treacherous there. I'll have to help you."

The man took off running.

Adam grabbed his pistol out of the holster. "Stay here!" He sprinted after his prisoner.

Chapter Three

Stay here? Was he worried that she'd run after the bad guy? It took courage to chase a man who'd pointed a pistol at you and made threats. She wasn't courageous. If she was, she would have fought harder after the auditor absolved her adoptive father of any wrongdoing in regards to her trust. She would have taken back what she believed he'd stolen from her. But she hadn't. She wouldn't. Because she was a coward. Being courageous and fighting back had never done her any good. It had only made things worse. So somewhere along the line, just giving in had become a habit.

Still, not at least checking on the ranger seemed wrong. So she kept moving forward, toward where he'd disappeared, even though she had no idea what she'd do if he needed help. She certainly hadn't done anything to help her best friend, the friend who was the only reason she'd survived her awful foster, later turned adoptive, family.

Where are you, Tracy? That man had to be lying. You have to be hiding somewhere, safe, not some thug's prisoner.

The curve where the ranger and his prisoner had disappeared loomed up ahead. What was the officer's name? Adam something. McKenzie, maybe? Yes, that was it. Cool name for a hot guy. Of course, she hadn't been thinking about his good looks during that frightening standoff. She'd stared up into those deep blue eyes and all she could think was that her friend Tracy was about to die, because of Jody's own stupidity. Her only chance to save her friend had been to lie, or so she'd thought. But she hadn't lied convincingly. She'd been too dang scared to pull it off.

Hysterical laughter bubbled up in her chest. Pull what off? What had she thought she could do? Convince a police officer that someone pointing a gun at someone else was no more significant than changing lanes on a highway without signaling? That Adam McKenzie would give them a warning and let them go on their merry way?

Once again, she'd had a choice to make. Once again, she'd made the wrong one. What she should have done was be honest, tell the ranger exactly what was going on. The time for going it alone had evaporated the second a man with scary tattoos had pulled a gun on her. What was she supposed to do now? If she told McKenzie the truth, would that sign Tracy's death warrant? Probably. Maybe. All she knew for sure was that Tracy needed help. But when help had arrived, in the form of a handsome, dark-haired ranger, she'd squandered the opportunity. And put him in danger, too.

Why hadn't he come back yet?

She stopped and peered down the trail, or what

was left of it. McKenzie hadn't exaggerated its haz-
ardous condition. She'd leaped over rock slides and
logs a dozen times as she'd run from the man with the
gun. He'd caught her, of course. Had she really thought
she'd get away? Just like one of those too-stupid-to-live
women in a horror movie, she'd run up the stairs instead
of out of the house. Or, in this case, up the trail instead
of back to her car.

Idiot. Stupid, cowardly idiot.

Her hands fisted at her sides. To be fair, she couldn't
have reached her car. He was standing in the way,
and there really had been nowhere else to go. Self-
recriminations weren't helping. She was in deep, deep
trouble and had no clue how to fix it, or even whether
it *could* be fixed. But she at least needed to try. Standing here, waiting, wasn't accomplishing anything. It
certainly wasn't finding her missing friend or saving
an officer who might be in trouble.

She took a hesitant step toward the curve, then another. Her hand itched for the security of her pistol. But,
of course, the one time she actually needed her gun it
was locked in the safe in her apartment. That decision,
at least, she couldn't feel bad about. There was no way
she could have predicted what would happen when she
drove up here in response to Tracy's text. That she might
be in danger had never entered her mind.

When she reached the curve, she squatted down by
the wall of rock and peered around the edge. Her stomach sank, as if she'd plummeted down a steep roller-
coaster drop. McKenzie no longer had his gun. Instead,
he stood about twenty feet away from her, hands in the

air. And directly in front of him was another man pointing a pistol directly at McKenzie's chest.

The man McKenzie had handcuffed was still cuffed. But he was leaning against a tree another ten feet beyond the ranger and the other gunman. His face bore an angry, impatient expression as he watched the standoff.

McKenzie shifted slightly, revealing some bloody cuts on the right side of his face. She drew a sharp breath. All three men jerked their heads toward her. She pressed a hand to her throat, belatedly realizing she must have made a sound.

"Nice of you to join us, Jody," the handcuffed man called out, his earlier cocky grin back in place. "Stay right where you are. Remember what I told you." He half turned, looking over his shoulder at the other gunman as he flexed his hands. "Owen, just get the dang keys already and get these things off me. Officer Mayberry can wait."

Jody swallowed, his earlier threats running through her mind. Somehow he'd gotten it into his head that she had something he wanted. And he was using Tracy as leverage. It stood to reason that she could do the opposite, couldn't she? Leverage whatever he thought she had in return for Tracy's safety? If she helped McKenzie, wouldn't the bad guy have to keep Tracy alive until he got what he wanted?

She curled her nails against her palms. Why was she even debating with herself? It wasn't like she could just run away. No matter what, she couldn't ignore the fact that Adam McKenzie was right here, unarmed and outnumbered, with a gun pointed at him. He needed help. She had to do something. But what could she do?

The man named Owen had keys in his left hand now, keys that he must have taken from McKenzie. His gaze stayed on the ranger as he trained the pistol on him and backed toward the tree.

McKenzie's gaze locked on Jody. He glanced to the right, toward the curve of rock wall and subtly jerked his head. Clearly, he wanted her to run up the path, to escape while she could.

She shook her head, even though she really, *really* wanted to give in to her cowardice and do exactly that—retreat, run, hide. But she'd just had this particular argument with herself. And lost.

His jaw clenched. He obviously wasn't happy with her response. He jerked his head again.

Ignoring his unspoken command, she studied the other two men. The one with the gun was fumbling with the set of keys. Their attention was temporarily diverted. McKenzie must have realized the same thing. He edged toward her. One foot. Two feet. When he was about ten feet away, he took off running toward her.

A shout sounded behind him. He grabbed Jody's arm and yanked her around the corner as more shouts and curses sounded.

"The cuffs, the cuffs! Hurry!" The handcuffed guy was apparently ordering Owen to remove the cuffs before they took off in pursuit.

"Go, go, go!" McKenzie's fingers tightened around her upper arm, pulling her up the trail. When a downed tree blocked their way, he lifted her up as if she weighed nothing and leaped over the tree. He set her on her feet and they took off again.

The *clomp-clomp* of boots pounding up the path sounded behind them. She looked over her shoulder. The first gunman didn't have his hands cuffed anymore. The short delay of removing them had given her and McKenzie a head start. But their lead was dwindling.

"Come on." McKenzie pulled her around rocks, over branches, at an impossibly fast pace.

"I'm trying," she gasped, struggling to match his long strides. She already knew she couldn't outrun the man behind them going uphill. She'd tried once and failed. Keeping up with the tall, long-legged McKenzie was impossible.

"Stop or we'll shoot!" the man named Owen yelled at them.

She started to look over her shoulder again. But McKenzie tugged her forward.

"Don't look back. It'll only slow you down." He yanked her around another curve in the trail.

A shot rang out. Jody instinctively ducked. But McKenzie was already pulling her under some thick branches from another downed tree. He came out the other side, hopped over more branches, then lifted her over.

A bullet whined past them. She let out a startled gasp and pressed a hand to her galloping heart. Good grief, that was close. McKenzie didn't react at all. Was the man used to getting shot at? He pulled her behind a huge boulder that was clustered with several others and pushed her down. He scanned the area around them, up the trail, out toward the open vista of mountains that alternated between blackened bald spots and new spring greenery poking up through the ashes.

The twin peaks of the Chimney Tops, two of the higher mountains in the park, stood out in stark relief from the destruction around them. She'd never even been in the park before, other than sitting in a car looking out the window as her adoptive father wheeled and dealed for yet another parcel of land. The only reason she recognized that particular landmark was because a new client had shown her pictures of them a few weeks ago and was considering hiring her to take new ones for a tourist brochure. What she didn't understand was why McKenzie was looking at the Chimney Tops. It wasn't like they had a helicopter and could magically fly to them and escape.

His gaze flicked back to her. "I need to know whether I can trust you."

The cuts on his face had guilt flooding through her. "I could have run when you told me to. But I didn't leave you behind. Isn't that proof enough?"

He seemed to consider that, then shrugged. "For now, *you're* going to have to trust *me*."

She gave a nervous laugh. "Well, I certainly don't trust the guys shooting at us. Where are they?" She tried to peek around the largest boulder. He stopped her with a hand on her shoulder.

"Don't. They've hunkered down behind the last tree we jumped over, about forty feet back. I imagine they're waiting to see if I'm going to pull a weapon from my backpack, since they made me toss my pistol into the ravine and took Tattoo Guy's pistol away from me."

Hope unfurled in her chest. "Do you? Have a backup gun?"

He shook his head. "I've got a hunting knife. But you know the saying about bringing a knife to a gunfight."

"I'm really good with a knife. I could throw it at them. All I'd need is some kind of diversion to get one of them to stand up and give me a clear target."

As soon as she said it, she realized she'd made a mistake. He was looking at her with open suspicion again.

"In college," she rushed to explain, "I hired a guy who ran a gun range to teach me to defend myself. He taught me to shoot. But he also taught me how to throw a knife."

"Ever thrown a knife at a real, live person?"

"No, of course not, but—"

Bam! Bam!

They both ducked at the shockingly loud sound of pistol fire.

She drew a shaky breath. "Well?" She held out her hand for the knife.

"I'm not giving up my only weapon just yet."

She dropped her hand. "You have a better suggestion?"

He looked toward the Chimney Tops again. "I'm considering a few possibilities."

"Is one of them to crouch down and use these boulders to block them from seeing us retreat up the path, back the way you came? We might be able to get pretty far up the trail before they realize we're gone."

"That's a good suggestion, except for one problem." He shrugged out of his backpack and unzipped the top. "The trail straightens out after that next curve, with no cover of any kind for about three hundred yards. It's also unstable. There's a lot of debris but nothing sizable enough to hide us from view. The odds of us making it that far before those guys work up the courage to storm our little hideout are too low to make it worth the risk." He pulled out a length of white nylon rope and the knife he'd mentioned earlier.

She was about to argue with him, but the rope made her pause. "What's the rope for?"

"So we don't die."

It took several seconds for her to realize he wasn't going to expand on his cryptic answer. Instead, he shoved the knife into a leather holder and tucked it into his backpack. After slipping the pack onto his shoulders, he connected some extra straps on the pack that he hadn't bothered to fasten earlier. One went over his chest. Two more attached the pack to his belt loops with metal clips. She thought they might be called carabiners, like she'd used when Tracy had badgered her into going on a zip-lining trip in Pigeon Forge to celebrate Jody's new, second job at Campbell Investigations.

"What are you doing?" she tried again.

He picked up the length of rope that he'd cut. His fingers fairly flew as he tied knots and created loops.

She watched him with growing frustration. The gunmen could be creeping up on them this very minute. So why was he tying knots? She hated being kept in the dark. Her life was on the line just as much as his.

And Tracy's.

He pulled on one of the loops as if testing it, then let out a few more inches, making it larger.

"Are you going to tie them up or try to lasso them or what?" she snapped, unable to hide her frustration any longer.

For the first time since he'd appeared on the trail with a goofy, dumb-as-a-rock grin, he gave her a genuine smile. It lit up his eyes and made him look years younger than the thirty-one or -two that she'd assumed him to be. Maybe he was only in his late twenties?

"Lasso them? Can't say that's ever been part of my law enforcement training. Might be a good skill to learn, though."

He continued to work the rope through the metal clips. "Hypothetical. We figure out a way to get Owen or Tattoo Guy to stand up and give us a clear target. You do a Wonder Woman move and take him out. That leaves the second thug with two pistols, and potentially other weapons we don't even know about. We're left without even a knife to defend ourselves. What would we do then?"

"Maybe I do another Wonder Woman move and lasso the second guy."

His lips twitched as if he was trying not to laugh. He looped the rope through one of the backpack's metal clips.

She curled her fingers against her thighs. It was either that or shake him. She closed her eyes for a moment and drew deep, calming breaths. Their lives were on the line and this man was pushing all her buttons. What she needed to do was calm down and think. There had to be something they could do instead of just waiting here playing with a rope. She opened her eyes again, then frowned. "What *are* you doing?"

He swept the ground between them clear of debris, scattering several broken pieces of branches and twigs, then motioned for her to move toward him. Exasperated, but curious enough to see if he actually had some kind of plan, she scooted toward him on her knees. He closed the distance and slid the rope through one of the belt loops on her shorts.

"McKenzie. What are—"

"Give me a minute."

She blew out an irritated breath and held her hands out of the way as he threaded the rope through all the loops on her shorts. When he was done, he tied the end of the rope to another metal loop on his backpack, effectively anchoring them to each other, with just a few feet in between.

"McKenzie?"

He tilted her chin up so she was looking into his eyes. "Is your name really Jody?"

She swallowed, her whole body flushing with heat when she realized just how close her breasts were to his chest, her lips to his. "Y…yes. Jody Vanessa Ingram." She hated that her voice came out a breathy whisper.

"Pretty name."

"Vanessa was my biological mom's name." Why had she said that? It didn't matter one bit under the circumstances.

He smiled. "Well, Jody Vanessa. We're about to explore one of those possibilities I mentioned earlier. And I think it's time you called me Adam. Don't you?"

His deep voice and cool blue eyes seemed to cast a spell on her. She couldn't think with him this close, could barely even breathe.

"Come on out from behind that rock and we won't kill you," Owen shouted. "All we want to do is talk."

She blinked. The spell was broken. Thank goodness. "McKenzie... I mean, Adam. What's the plan here? Why did you—"

He tugged the rope, pulling them even closer together. "This is where that trust part comes into play."

She licked her suddenly dry lips. "I'm not sure what you—"

He grabbed one of the short, broken pieces of branch that he'd swept out of the way earlier and tossed it over the top of the boulder.

Boom! The stick exploded into sawdust.

Jody ducked down, even though she was already behind the boulder.

Adam winced but didn't duck. "They're better shots than I'd hoped. This is going to be close."

"Close? What are you—"

He grabbed her around the waist.

She read the truth in his eyes and suddenly realized what he was going to do. The rope. The fact that he'd tied the two of them together. Him staring out at the Chimney Tops and telling her she needed to trust him. Her stomach lurched, and she pushed against his chest, to no avail. He didn't budge and the rope wouldn't have let her move very far anyway. "No. No, no, no. *Please*. I can't do this. I'm too scared. I *can't*."

Sympathy filled his gaze. He brushed a featherlight caress down the side of her face. "Then I'll just have to do it for both of us." He grabbed two more sticks and threw them high into the air. Shots rang out. He yanked her forward, clasping her tightly against his chest as he raced in a crouch behind the boulders toward where the trail disappeared over the edge of the mountain.

"No!" she cried, desperately pushing against him. "Please!"

The gunmen shouted.

Adam yanked her forward. She screamed as they tumbled over the cliff.

Chapter Four

They hit the ground hard, a tangle of arms and legs flopping end over end. Jody's head snapped against Adam's chest. Blood filled her mouth. She was too busy trying to grab a tree, a root, anything to stop their out-of-control roll down the steep mountainside to even cry out in pain.

"Hold on," his voice rumbled next to her ear as his arms squeezed her against his chest.

She caught a glimpse of another steep drop, then sucked in a startled breath and closed her eyes. Shots rang out from somewhere above them as they plummeted into open space again.

We're going to die.

Strong arms clasped her so tightly she thought her body would break in two. Then she hit something hard—or he did, because she was on top of him. Their entwined bodies bounced several more times and slid a heart-stopping few more yards. Then, just as suddenly as their wild flight had begun, it was over. His chest rose and fell beneath hers, his ragged breaths fanning against the top of her head. But other than that, and her own gasping breaths, the world was blessedly still.

We didn't die.

Yet.

Her eyes flew open. Miraculously, her glasses had somehow survived the tumble down the mountain and were still on. Which gave her a startlingly clear view of a pair of brilliant blue eyes staring directly into hers from just inches away. It was only then that she realized just how intimately she was pressed against him. Her breasts were crushed to his chest, her cleavage straining the top of her lacy bra, her blouse having surrendered several buttons. Her right thigh was sandwiched between both of his legs, pressing against a very warm spot that left little to the imagination about just how well-proportioned he was to his taller-than-average height. Her cheeks flaming, she tried to scramble off him.

"Hold it, wait." His harsh whisper had her going still as his hands tightened on her arms. He tilted his head back and looked up the mountain they'd just tumbled down, apparently searching for the gunmen.

Her gaze followed his. She didn't see anyone. But what she did see had her shaking again. How they'd managed to fall so far through such rough terrain without being killed was a mystery. As she noticed the deep skid and slide marks down the grassy and rocky terrain, and the broken tree branches that marked their path, she realized that maybe it wasn't such a mystery after all. Her benefactor had rolled and tugged and pulled her to him the entire ride down. That was the only thing that explained how they hadn't crashed into boulders and trees and been killed. He'd done that. He'd protected both of them.

Or he'd protected *her*, at least.

Her eyes filled with tears as she realized just what his noble actions had cost him. Blood was drying on his face from his earlier cuts, likely from an altercation or ambush by the second gunman, the one named Owen. More blood streaked his arms and neck. A long gash marred his left biceps, blood trickling from a wound that was smeared with dirt. A black shadow was already darkening on his forehead where he'd obviously smacked it against something. And her? Other than a bitten tongue, dirty and torn clothes, and a few stinging minor cuts on her arms and legs, she was unharmed.

"You're hurt," she said. "I'm so sorry. Do you have a first-aid kit in your backpack? I can dress your wounds."

His gaze shot to hers. "Are you okay? You're crying."

The concern in his voice as he reached a hand toward her had shame and guilt flaring up inside. She jerked back to scramble off him but slammed down against his chest because of the rope that still connected them.

"Sorry, sorry. Dang it." She wiped the tears away and tried to tug the rope free.

"Here, let me." His deep voice was soft again, gentle, as he pressed the carabiners on each side of his pack. A few quick tugs on the knots and they seemed to magically unravel. Another yank and the slick nylon rope pulled free from her belt loops.

She pressed against the ground on either side of his chest and pushed herself up off him, then sat back on her heels and yanked the ends of her blouse back together to cover her bra.

"Are you okay?" he asked again, sitting up.

She nodded. "Thanks to you, I'm fine. But you're not." She waved toward the dozens of cuts on his arms, his face. "You took the brunt of the fall to protect me. Why would you do that?"

He frowned as if in confusion. "Why wouldn't I? It's my job."

She shook her head, unable to fathom such selfless thinking. "First-aid kit?"

"Later." He pushed to his knees and looked up again. "I don't see our two friends."

She followed his gaze to the cliff, which seemed impossibly far away. She still couldn't believe they'd rolled down the mountain and hadn't gotten killed, or shot, or both. But thankfully the gunmen weren't standing there, aiming a pistol at them.

"Why aren't they still up there, trying to shoot us?" she asked. "Maybe they didn't think we'd survive the drop?" She shivered and wrapped her hands around her waist. "Maybe they're worried someone heard the shots, so they took off?"

He shook his head. "Unless there are more trespassers ignoring the trail-closed signs, there's no one else to hear the gunshots. And I don't see our friends just moseying to their car and heading back where they came from after all the trouble they went to. They're after something. And they don't have it yet." His eyes stared deep into hers, once again darkening with suspicion.

"How much motivation do they have, Jody? Enough to figure out a way down that mountain to come after us?"

A cold chill shot through her. She looked up again. But the only thing above them was a bright blue sky and a hawk gliding over the mountaintops.

"Jody? Who were those men? Why are they after you?" He climbed to his feet and helped her stand.

She stepped back so she could meet his gaze without getting a crick in her neck. "You're bleeding. I really think we should get the first aid kit." She took another step back.

He grabbed her waist and yanked her to the side. "Haven't you ever been in the mountains before? Never back up without looking first."

She glanced over her shoulder and sucked in a breath. The blood seemed to drain from her body, leaving her cold and shaking. Once again, she'd been close to the edge of another drop-off and had nearly plunged over the side.

Swallowing hard, she pressed a shaking hand to her throat. "Thank you. You've saved me more times than I can count and we've known each other for less than an hour."

"We need to go." He put a hand to the small of her back and urged her toward the charred woods to their right.

"Go where? It looks like we're heading toward another cliff." She tried to stop, but his hand was firm, pushing her forward.

"We'll make our own path. We have to. Out here

we're too much in the open." He held back a branch on a new sapling that had sprouted from the destruction.

They rounded a curve in the mountain, the going steep, treacherous, with loose rocks underfoot. A few yards farther and they were surrounded by trees, half of them scorched but miraculously still standing. Some of them supported canopies of new growth in spite of their blackened trunks. The underbrush had resurged here. Many of the bushes were taller than both of them.

Far below, water gurgled and rushed over boulders. She caught glimpses of it through breaks in the trees. Rocks in the middle of the stream created eddies and little rapids. The artist in her craved a few moments to stand there and gape at the beauty below, to frame it in her mind's eye like she'd frame a camera shot. But the reality of their situation, and the imposing ranger beside her, had her hurrying as fast as she could manage through the rough terrain.

He took the outside, near the steep drop, using the rise of the mountain as a barrier against her falling over the edge. His gaze was never still. He constantly scanned the woods around them, looking up at the mountain that rose above their heads. His constant vigilance should have made her feel secure. Instead, it only reminded her of the danger they were in.

She finally grabbed one of the saplings they were passing and used it as an anchor in the sea of fear that threatened to pull her under. "Wait."

He stopped beside her, brows raised in question.

"Your arms—some of the cuts are still bleeding. And

they need to be cleaned so they don't get infected. Do you have medical supplies in your pack?"

"You're stalling, Jody. We need to get moving."

She waved a hand toward the trees surrounding them. "Unless those gunmen take a swan dive over a cliff or have billy goat ancestors, I don't see how they could follow us. It's too steep and rocky."

"They don't have to get too close. They just need one clear shot. Up on the trail, we were jumping over downed trees and weaving around curves. Plus, their adrenaline was probably pumping pretty good. Otherwise they wouldn't have missed. I don't want to hang around in one spot and give them a perfect target."

Her hand tightened around the sapling. "You're not helping."

He frowned again. "Helping with what?"

She huffed out an impatient breath. "I'm scared, okay? Right now I'm more afraid of plunging headfirst over a cliff again than some gunmen who may or may not be following us."

His expression softened. "I wish I didn't have to force you to keep going. But I don't see those guys giving up that easily."

She swallowed. "Why do you say that?"

"Because they thought nothing of trying to shoot a federal officer. Your average thug thinks twice in a situation like that. They don't want to risk bringing the wrath of the feds down on them. But our guys not only shot at us multiple times, they risked their own lives running up a dangerous trail to do it. My guess is they might lie low for a little while to see whether backup arrives. But not for long. Then they'll be looking for a way to hike down here and find us."

He motioned toward the radio hooked to his belt. "I've turned this thing on half a dozen times since our flight down the mountain. There's no signal, not even a burst of static. One of the radio towers was destroyed in the wildfires. What we have to do is get within range of another tower so we can radio for help. Until then, we keep going." He arched a brow. "Unless you can tell me why those men might decide to hightail it out of here without finishing us off. Just what are they after? Who are they?"

She hesitated.

His jaw tightened. "Jody—"

"I don't know their names, other than the one calling the other Owen in front of both of us."

"You're splitting hairs. Not knowing their full names and not knowing what they want are two very different things. You were arguing with the first man when I approached. He later warned you to remember what he'd told you. What were you arguing about? What did he want you to remember?"

Without waiting for her reply, he pried her hand from the tree and tugged her through the woods.

Her foot skidded on some loose rocks. She let out a yelp, but he grabbed her around the waist and steadied her before she could fall.

"I've got you," he said. "Try not to worry. My boots hold the trail a lot better than your sneakers. I'm not going to let anything happen to you, okay?"

His voice was gentle again. But there was an underlying thread of steel. He wanted answers. And he deserved them. Even if it meant she might go to jail, or at the least, have all her career aspirations ruined. All those years of college, the sacrifices she'd made, the two jobs she was holding down were for nothing. In one stupid week, she'd destroyed it all.

She jerked to a halt, pressing a hand to her throat. "I can't believe how selfish I'm being, thinking about my future career and prison when Tracy's missing." She moved her hand to her stomach. "That's just the kind of thing my adoptive father would do." She squeezed her eyes shut. "I think I'm going to be sick."

"Your career? Prison? Wait, who's Tracy?"

Chapter Five

Jody groaned and whirled around, gagging as she dropped to her knees and emptied the contents of her stomach.

Suddenly a strong arm was around her waist and a gentle hand swept her hair back from her face, holding it loosely behind her as Adam spoke soothing words in her ear. She was too sick and miserable to protest his help. The spasms wouldn't seem to stop and she started dry heaving.

"Deep breaths," he said. "Slow, deep breaths. You'll be okay. Slow and easy."

Somehow the sound of his voice calmed her. She dragged in a deep breath, then another. The knots in her stomach eased, and she could finally breathe normally without feeling like her stomach was trying to kill her.

Her world suddenly tilted as he scooped her up into his arms. Before she could even ask him what he was doing, he'd set her down several feet away beneath the branches of a thick stand of trees. The realization that he was giving them cover in case the bad guys were around had her stomach clenching with dread. She pressed a hand to her belly.

"This should help." A bottle of water and a wet cloth appeared as if by magic as he handed them to her from the backpack he'd been carrying.

She rinsed her mouth out and spit. After a long drink, she washed her face with the cloth.

"Better?" He was on his knees in front of her, his brow furrowed with concern.

"Better. Thank you." She swept her hair back from her shoulders. Heat flushed her skin at the realization of what had just happened. She groaned and covered her face. "I can't believe you witnessed that. And that you helped me. I'm so embarrassed."

He tugged her hands down. "Jody, what made you so upset? Who's Tracy? Is she in trouble?"

She nodded miserably. "I think so. She texted me. That's why I was on the trail. Well, partly, anyway. I mean, I was in the parking lot. But she wasn't there, so I checked the bathrooms, and when I came out, that guy was there…and he started toward me. I saw his gun sticking out of his pocket, so I ran. I just ran. Then he was there, on the trail, with the gun—"

"Take a breath." He took one of her hands in his. "Back up. Who is Tracy?"

A ragged breath shuddered out of her. "My sister." She waved her hand. "Not a real sister. She's my friend. My very best friend. I don't have any biological siblings, just adoptive sisters and brothers. Not that I'm knocking adoptive families in general. I think they can be wonderful, for other people. But it hasn't turned out so well for me. We don't exactly visit each other or exchange Christmas cards." She drew a deep breath. "Tracy is not part of my adoptive family. She's my friend, my best friend, more of a sister to me than my adoptive sisters ever were. And her family is more of a family to me than my adoptive one." She closed her eyes and fisted her hands against the tops of her thighs.

"Tattoo Guy, he did something to her? To Tracy?"

She nodded and looked at him. "He abducted her. At least, that's what he told me. I didn't know, or I swear I would have called the police. I would never do anything to risk her life." She pressed her hand to her throat. "I think I may have just killed her. By running, with you. I shouldn't have done that." She squeezed her eyes shut again.

"Jody, I need you to be strong. For your friend, okay? I know it's hard. But you have to hold it together so we can figure out what to do. All right?"

She nodded and opened her eyes. "Okay. I'm sorry."

"Nothing to apologize for. I'm going to ask you some questions and I need you to give me the answers. Short and to the point. And we need to keep moving while we talk." He pulled her to her feet. "Can you do that?"

"I'll try. Yes. I'm sorry." She grimaced. "I know. Quit saying that."

He smiled and pulled her with him through the trees. "What's Tracy's full name?"

"Larson. Her name is Tracy Larson."

"Is she your age?"

"Yes. Twenty-four. We went to school together, from grade school through high school. She didn't go to col-

lege. I went to TSU, Tennessee State University, I...
Sorry. Short and to the point. I forgot. Sorry."

"It's okay. I went to TSU, too. When's the last time
you saw her?"

She patted her pocket to check the time of Tracy's
last text messages on her phone. But her pocket was
empty. They all were. "My phone and keys are gone."
She shook her head. "I know. Doesn't matter. I think
the last I heard from her was at work yesterday. She's
full-time. I'm part-time. I left at my usual two o'clock."

He steered her around a downed tree. "Friday at
2:00 p.m.? You're sure?"

"Pretty sure. I'm not counting the fake text this
morning. The guy with the gun must have sent that.
He tricked me."

"We'll get to that in a second. Are you sure you didn't
talk to Tracy on the phone after 2:00 p.m.?"

"Talk?"

His mouth quirked up in a smile. "Forgive me. I'm
a doddering thirty-year-old who actually uses phones
for spoken conversations. Let me rephrase. Did you text
each other? Share anything on social media?"

She surprised herself by laughing, which seemed ob-
scene given the situation. She quickly sobered. "Sorry.
But the idea of you being described as doddering is ridiculous. Trust me, most women my age would count
themselves lucky to be with a guy as smokin' hot as
you."

Her face flushed with heat as soon as the words left
her mouth. She absolutely refused to look at him. "Text,
yes, we texted a few times. Nothing seemed out of the

norm. Then, this morning, I got a new text from her saying she needed to meet me, that it was urgent. She said she'd be waiting in the parking lot at the Sugarland Mountain trailhead. I went to the visitor center, and her car wasn't there. I texted her to ask where she was, and she said in the parking lot on the other end of the trail, not the visitor center. So I headed there. Only, when I got there, her car wasn't there, either."

Tears burned the backs of her eyes, but she refused to give in to the urge to cry again. She swallowed against her tight throat and continued. "There were a couple of cars besides mine on the other side of the lot. One of them was a minivan with a family and kids. I didn't see anyone in the other car, a black Charger. Not then. The family went to use the public facilities by the beginning of the trail. Tracy texted back that she'd be there in a few minutes and to wait. I ducked into the restroom, chatted with some of the people from the minivan. They left before me. When I came out, they were just pulling out of the parking lot. That's when he got out of the car."

"Who? The guy with the tattoos?"

"Yes. I started toward my car, then stopped. He was walking really fast, straight toward me. But there wasn't anyone else around. And the men's restrooms were on the other side of the lot. There was no reason for him to be hurrying toward me. I don't know how to explain it. But he gave me the creeps, and he was between me and my car. I didn't want to let him get too close. So I walked toward the trail. I looked over my shoulder, and that's when I saw the gun." She swallowed. "He had a pistol sticking out of his pants pocket. I ran. I hopped over the cattle gate blocking the trail and took off. And he took off after me."

"Did he fire the gun?"

She frowned. "No. No, he never did. Not until you and I were running up the trail later."

He nodded as if that made sense to him. "Go on. You ran. Then what happened?"

"I used to run track in high school. I was pretty fast. But I'm not used to running up mountains or having to hop over downed trees. I couldn't sprint and pull away like I would in a flat footrace. He caught up to me right where you saw us. And he…he pointed his gun at me. And he…" She drew a ragged breath.

"You're doing great, Jody. Slow, deep breaths. What did he do next? What did he say to you?"

As much as she wanted to be strong for her friend, she was having a hard time holding back her terror. What was happening to Tracy right now? What had that man done to her? Was she even alive or had he lied to her?

"Jody. What did the man do when he caught you on the trail?" He steered her around a particularly rocky section and past some thorny shrubs.

She murmured her thanks and straightened. She could do this. She had to. For Tracy's sake. "He told me I had something of his and he wanted it. He said if I didn't give it to him, he would…he would kill Tracy." In spite of her efforts to stay calm, tears tracked down her cheeks. "He had her phone, showed it to me. That's how I knew he was telling the truth. He must have texted me to meet him there, pretending he was her. No way could he have gotten her phone without taking it from her. That thing is practically attached at her hip."

He pulled her to a halt and grasped her shoulders. "What do you have that he wants?"

"I don't have anything. I swear. He insisted I have pictures, maybe a video, or knew where they were. He said my boss had seen something he shouldn't have and that there was a gap in the time stamps on the pictures."

"Your boss?"

"Sam Campbell. He's a private investigator. Tracy and I work for him." She looked away, panic swelling inside her again. She'd been so stupid. So very, very stupid.

"You know what he's after, don't you?" The thread of steel was back in his voice.

She glanced up at him and wiped at the tears on her cheeks. "Not specifically, no. I assume that Sam performed surveillance on him, that he's one of Sam's clients. But all of Sam's pictures and videos are locked up at the office. I told him that. He shook his head, said that he'd searched there already. That's when we heard you whistling. He told me to keep my mouth shut, that Tracy would die if I told you anything."

His eyes widened. "You lied to me up on the trail to get me to leave you two alone, knowing he had a gun? If I'd bought your story, you would have been all alone with him. He could have killed you."

"I know. Looking back, it was stupid. But I didn't know what else to do. Tracy—" Her voice broke.

"You thought he would kill her if you didn't do what he told you. You risked your life for her. Whatever happens, you can't blame yourself. You did what you could."

She shook her head. "No. I was stupid, too scared to think straight. You don't make deals with criminals. What I should have done was shove him or something when you came up and yelled a warning." Her hand shook as she raked her hair back from her face. "You could have been killed."

He frowned. "Is that why you came looking for me after I chased Tattoo Guy down the trail? You were trying to save me?"

She snorted. "Fat lot of good it did. I just slowed you down. And now you're all scratched up and out here with me, without a weapon, with a couple of thugs possibly coming after us. I'm such an idiot."

His warm, strong hand gently urged her chin up so she had to look at him.

She pushed his hand away. "Go ahead. Yell at me. My stupidity has probably gotten my friend killed and nearly got you killed. Every decision I made was wrong. You'd have thought I would have learned better at college."

"What do you mean?"

"I studied criminal justice, graduated with honors. Not that it means I have any sense. Might as well tear up that piece of paper."

He frowned. "Aren't you being a bit hard on yourself? You drove up here because a friend said she needed you. A man chased you with a gun, threatened to kill your friend if you didn't do what he said. And as soon as you had a chance to escape, instead, you went *toward* trouble, to help a law enforcement officer you thought was in need. From where I stand, that's pretty darn amazing."

She blinked. "What?"

"You have the education, but not the training or the experience. And you're a civilian, unarmed. You did the best you could. I can't find fault with any of your decisions."

"Th…thank you?"

He smiled. "Come on. There are a lot of gaps in your story, like why someone with a criminal justice degree is working part-time as a private investigator." He tugged her hand, then stopped and looked over his shoulder at her when she pulled back. "Jody?"

"I'm not a private investigator," she confessed. "And when I tell you the rest, you aren't going to think I did the best I could or made good decisions. I didn't."

He turned to face her. "Go on."

"Tracy pretty much runs the office. I guess you'd call her an administrative assistant. I help Sam with his cases. But I'm not a licensed investigator, just a recent criminal justice grad trying to get some experience to help me get the job I really want—as a criminal investigator with the prosecutor's office. But those jobs are few and far between, so I'm working two jobs to make ends meet and trying to get a step up on the competition when the job I want opens up."

She waved her hand again. "Anyway, my point is that I'm his gofer, his researcher. Sometimes I interview clients and things like that. Sam does all the heavy lifting, and I take care of the grunt work."

He studied her intently, as if weighing her every word. "So far I'm not hearing any bad decisions or things for you to be worried about."

She tightened her hands into fists by her sides. "There's more. I screwed up. I mean, really, really screwed up." She let out a shaky breath and met his gaze again. "Sam disappeared a week ago. And before you ask, no, it's not unusual. He's had a tough time since his wife died of ovarian cancer about a year ago. He hits the bottle too hard. He usually shows up a few days later and will be fine for a while." She clenched her fists so hard the nails dug into her palms. "We always cover for him when he's on a binge. Do you understand what I'm telling you? He could lose his license if clients complain that he's a drunk and messes up cases. And besides that, if he messes up the cases, the income stops rolling in. And, well, Tracy and I both rely on that income. We live paycheck to paycheck. No paycheck means no food, no rent."

He stared at her intently. "You did more than run errands, didn't you?"

She nodded. "We may have…pretended to be Sam to some of the clients, through correspondence in the mail…to close out cases, resolve issues."

"You operated as PIs without a license. You're worried that you may have committed fraud. Even worse, mail fraud. That's a felony."

She winced and looked away.

The silence stretched out between them.

"Jody. There's more, isn't there?"

She nodded slowly.

His sigh could have knocked over a tree. "Go on. Might as well tell me the rest."

She swallowed, then forced herself to meet his gaze. Surprisingly, it wasn't the cold, judgmental look she'd expected. Instead, he looked at her with something far worse.

Pity.

She stiffened her spine and confessed the rest of her sins.

"Sam is dead. Tracy and I killed him."

Chapter Six

Adam dropped his chin to his chest and shook his head. If for even one second he thought Jody was telling the truth, he'd have pulled out his second set of handcuffs and Mirandized her. But in spite of her low opinion of herself, she struck him as painfully honest. In the span of a few hours, she'd confessed more to him than most people confessed to their priests. This young woman didn't know how to lie convincingly, as proven by the fiasco up on the trail. And she'd apologized at least a dozen times in the past few minutes, and meant it. She was riddled with guilt over things she shouldn't even feel guilty about. No way had she murdered someone.

"Okay," he said. "Tell me how you two did the dirty deed. Poison? Butcher knife? Machete?"

"Are you seriously making fun of me?"

He raised his head and gave her a baleful glance. "Are you seriously going to try to convince me you murdered someone?"

"Well, not directly, we didn't. But we might as well have. When Sam disappeared, we should have gone to the police, filled out a missing-persons report and—"

"Which the police would have set aside. They would have told you to give it a few more days because there was no evidence of foul play and your boss has a history of going off on drinking binges."

She crossed her arms, her mouth drawn into a tight line.

"Am I wrong? You said he disappeared all the time."

"That's not fair to Sam. He's a great man, more of a father to me than my adoptive father ever was. He doesn't disappear *all* the time. Just sometimes. And it's not like I think we should have reported it the first morning he didn't show up. There was no reason to think anything was wrong. But he's never been gone a whole week before. We should have done something on day five instead of…of…committing fraud. And then maybe Sam would be okay."

Everything about her posture and her tone told him she truly felt responsible. And he hadn't missed the hurt look in her eyes the last time she'd met his gaze. Which was several minutes ago. Now she was staring off into the woods, her pretty face mottled, her jaw tight. She was obviously upset, both because she took the weight of the world on her shoulders and because he'd made light of her claims. She'd really be angry if she knew how hard he was struggling not to laugh, or at least not to smile.

He cocked his head, studying her profile. She'd been through a traumatic experience. Her boss was missing—even though Adam was inclined to think the man would show up alive and well with a wicked hangover. Adam had met Sam Campbell a few times over the years and was well-acquainted with his reputation around town for going on occasional drinking binges—even before his wife's death. Not that Jody apparently knew that. His employees were trying to hide a secret that wasn't even a secret.

But Jody's best friend was *really* missing. And Tracy Larson was *not* likely to show up alive and well. Jody had been chased, threatened, shot at, pulled off a cliff—all in all the kind of morning that would crush most civilians. But here she stood, her back ramrod straight, her mouth compressed into a mutinous line as she glared her hurt feelings at the mountains around them.

And his teasing, his refusal to take her seriously had only added to her burden.

His shoulders slumped. He'd handled this all wrong. He started to apologize but stopped. What was he supposed to say? *Sorry I didn't believe that you could kill someone in cold blood*? She seemed so young in so many ways. At twenty-four, she was only six years younger than him. His last girlfriend had been younger, twenty-three. But Brandy had been just as bruised by the world and jaded as he was. The years between them hadn't mattered. This girl didn't seem world-weary or jaded and he didn't get the impression that she realized just how horrible or cruel people could sometimes be.

She crossed her arms, the movement pushing up her small breasts in the delicate, lacy bra that her torn blouse did little to conceal. His body's reaction to that innocent display surprised him. He could feel himself tightening, heat pulsing through his veins. And he had to admit, now that he *really* looked at her for the first time since this had all started, there was nothing girl-ish about her figure.

She was all woman, from her luscious red hair that bounced around her shoulders to the full, pink lips that gave her mouth a pouty, sultry look to her narrow waist that begged for a man's hands to span its narrow curves. Her legs weren't long and lean like Brandy's had been. But on Jody, her short, toned, silky-looking legs were the perfect complement to the rest of her. Even those green glasses on her perky nose were cute. All in all, she was one sexy package. And now that he'd finally noticed, he was cursing himself for the lust that shot through him. Jody needed a protector, not some guy drooling after her.

He forced his gaze back to her face and cleared his throat.

She arched a brow and looked at him in question, the hurt and anger still broadcast in her expression like a neon sign flashing at him. If she ever played poker, she'd lose every round. The art of bluffing was beyond her. Which was, all in all, refreshing. Most people he knew were great liars and couldn't be trusted. He had a feeling he could trust Jody in any situation, and she wouldn't let him down.

Maybe it was time he told her that. And confessed his own half-truths he'd tossed out earlier.

"You didn't sign your boss's name on anything you mailed, did you?"

She frowned. "No, why?"

"Then it's unlikely you committed fraud. All you did was manage the office, continue to send your boss's mail for him, tie up loose ends—stuff administrative assistants do for their bosses every day of the week all over the world. Unless you actually went up to someone and claimed to be a private investigator, you can let that guilt go. You didn't do anything wrong."

"But—"

"But nothing." He squeezed her hand. "I'm sorry I didn't treat your concerns more seriously earlier. You've been through a lot, and you're worried about your boss and your friend. I should have been a better listener and commiserated more."

She cleared her throat. "Well, maybe. But I was being a bit over-the-top when I said we'd killed Sam. It's just that I'm really worried about him. I wish I'd done something more when he didn't show up. Now, with Tracy missing, and that creepy man with the gun thinking Sam had more pictures of him somewhere, I can't help worrying everything's connected and both Tracy and Sam are either in real trouble or—"

"Leave the 'or' to me, okay? That's my job, to worry about stuff like that." He tugged her forward and they started through the woods again. "Let's focus on getting you to safety and then I'll work with the local police to start an investigation and search for your friend. If I were a betting man, I'd bet you that Sam is alive and well, passed out on his couch at home. And your friend is alive, too."

Her hand tightened in his. "You really think so?"

"I do," he lied, seeing no point in making her even more miserable. "And as long as Tattoo Guy thinks you have something he needs, he won't hurt Tracy. He needs her as leverage. His threats up on the trail were a complete bluff."

She stopped, and he did, too, facing her.

"Why do you think it was a bluff?"

"Because he didn't shoot you. In the parking lot, you said he chased you up the trail, then confronted you. If he'd wanted to kill you, he could have. Instead, he threatened you, threatened your friend's life, to get you to talk. To tell him where the pictures are that he thinks are floating around somewhere. That's your bargaining chip. As long as he thinks you have something he needs, he'll keep Tracy safe as leverage."

"Then…those were just warning shots? He wouldn't really shoot us?"

Adam laughed harshly. "Oh no. He'll kill me the first chance he gets. No doubt. And his type, he'll hurt you in a heartbeat. Might even try to shoot you in the leg or bust your kneecap to get you to talk. Or worse." He forced a smile he was far from feeling when he saw the worry in her eyes. "Which is why we don't want to risk him catching up to us if he wasn't smart enough to head back to his car and hightail it out of here."

A deep rumble sounded in the distance.

They both looked up at the sky. Instead of the brilliant blue it had been earlier, it was rapidly turning dark and ominous with heavy rainclouds blowing in to cover the sun.

"A storm's rolling in. And we aren't anywhere near the next cell tower yet to radio for someone to get us out of here before the lightning show starts."

"That's crazy. There was no hint of an oncoming storm a few minutes ago."

"Oh, I'm sure there were hints. We were just more focused on watching out for thugs than keeping an eye on the weather." He studied the terrain around them, then pointed off to the right. "There, see how the mountain forms a natural depression over there? Away from trees or rocks that will conduct electricity? That's the safest place around here to hunker down when the lightning starts. Won't keep us dry in the rain, but it's safer than being under trees or becoming human lightning rods out here in the open like we are now. Let's go."

He motioned for her to join him and led her down a steeper descent than they'd been taking before. He hadn't wanted to risk her twisting an ankle or getting scraped up on the rocks if she lost her footing, so he'd been leading her around the mountain, taking a more gradual slope down toward the valley below. But storms up here could be deadly. There was no time to waste.

Sure enough, her sneakers weren't up to the task of navigating the rocky path. She wobbled and skittered across some loose stones, her arms flailing as she tried to maintain her balance. He grabbed her waist, steadying her.

"Next time you hike in the mountains, wear some decent shoes," he teased.

She smiled up at him. And it did crazy things to his breathing.

He swallowed and urged her forward again. The breeze that had kicked up helped cool his body and bring clarity to his thoughts. They really did need to find shelter, fast, or they could get struck by lightning, or even drown in a flash flood if they were crossing one of the dry creek beds when the rains started.

Boom!

Jody looked up at the sky. Adam tackled her, wrapping his arms protectively around her as they both fell to the ground. He heard her gasp of pain when they landed, the breath leaving her in a whoosh as her chin smacked his chest. The back of his head snapped against a rock, practically making his teeth rattle.

She shoved against him. "What was that for? The thunder—"

"It wasn't thunder. Move, move, move!" He rolled and grabbed her around the waist, yanking her up with him in a crouch.

Boom! Boom!

A chunk of rock exploded inches from Adam's head.

Jody let out a startled yelp and looked over her shoulder. "Was that—"

"Gunfire!" He shoved her in front of him, shielding her body with his. "Run, Jody. Run!"

Chapter Seven

Chh-chh.

The ominous sound didn't have to be explained. Jody had heard it dozens of times in action movies. It was the sound of a shotgun being pumped.

Adam was already pulling her to the ground before she could react.

Boom! Chh-chh. Boom!

Leaves and sawdust rained down on them from the tree above. Jody let out a squeak of fear before she could stop herself. She started to push off the ground to run again, but Adam pressed her back down.

He held his fingers to his mouth, signaling her to be quiet, then pointed to his right and motioned for her to precede him.

She nodded to let him know she understood, even though she wanted to yell at him for always making himself a human target to protect her. It wasn't right, regardless of what his job title might be. But arguing would only make him more of a target as the men pursuing them homed in on the sounds.

Her bare knees screamed in protest as she half

crawled, half duckwalked through the woods, behind clumps of bushes and trees, toward another group of boulders. She tried to avoid dried leaves, twigs, anything that could crunch or snap and give away their location. But everything in this half-burned section of the mountains seemed to make noise when she touched it. All she could do was hope the sound didn't carry to the men chasing them. Their only chance was to give them the slip, find a hiding place and hunker down.

A hand tapped her shoulder. She looked back at Adam. He held up one finger, pointed off to their left and then held his hands out together as if he were holding a shotgun. Her stomach sank, but she nodded in understanding. He held up a finger again and pointed a little farther to the left, almost behind them. This time he held his other hand out, pointer finger extended, thumb raised, in an imitation of a handgun. He must have seen Owen and Tattoo Guy, both closing in on them. One of them had a pistol. How had the other one gotten a shotgun? Had they hidden one in the woods, just in case the threat about Tracy failed? In case Jody managed to escape and they had to give chase?

She nodded, again letting him know she understood. Then she held her hands out in a gesture of helplessness and mouthed, "What do we do now?"

He pointed to the right and once again held both his hands out as if he were holding a shotgun, or maybe a rifle. She bit her lip to keep from crying out in frustration. At least now she knew where Tattoo Guy and Owen had gotten a shotgun. A third man was after them. He must have been a reinforcement, and he'd brought more weapons.

Please don't let there be a fourth thug out here with yet another gun.

He pointed to her, then himself, then motioned behind him. She frowned. That couldn't be right. He wanted them to go back the way they'd already come? She shook her head and pointed straight in front of them, a direct line that would keep the two guys to their left and the other to the right.

His brows drew down, and he shook his head. "Trust me," he mouthed silently. "Come on."

She didn't protest when he grasped her shoulders and turned her around. All she could do was put her faith in him and, as he'd told her, trust him. He was the professional, and she presumed he knew his way around this mountain. She sure didn't.

Her instincts screamed at her to jump up and run. It would be much faster. The ground was almost level in this section of the mountain. They'd descended to a valley or a plateau, perfect for stretching out her legs and putting on a burst of speed and stamina that would take her far away from this place in no time. Years of running, both in school and out, would finally come in handy—if Adam would give her the chance. As long as she didn't have to run an obstacle course—leaping over rocks and trees that had slowed her down on the trail above them—she was confident she could outrun these thugs.

But she couldn't outrun a bullet.

Feeling all kinds of wrong about it, she did as Adam

directed. Half crawling, half walking in a deep crouch, turning left or right each time he thumped her on one of her shoulders from behind to let her know which direction to go.

It seemed like an eternity had passed by the time he tugged her hair in what she assumed was his way of telling her to stop. The man was treating her like a horse with his tapping and hair pulling. She wanted to scream in frustration. Instead, she looked over her shoulder and arched a brow to ask him what to do next. But he wasn't looking at her. He was staring off into the woods, eyes narrowed, every muscle tense and alert. He reminded her of a panther: stealthy, alert, searching for prey. Except that in this case, she and Adam were the prey. They were the ones being hunted.

His eyes widened, and he suddenly grabbed her waist, hauling her backward with him. She scrabbled with her feet, pushing back to help him. Once they were behind a downed tree, he shoved her onto the ground and covered her with his body.

Good grief, he was heavy. About six feet, three inches of pure muscle squashed her into the dirt, the musty smell of pine needles and wet moss seeping into her lungs. Drawing a deep breath was impossible, so she breathed shallowly, one after the other, struggling to get enough oxygen.

The sharp crack of a snapping twig sounded close by. She froze. Adam pressed her even harder into the ground, and it dawned on her that he had dark clothes on and she had a white blouse. In the gloom of this part of the forest, her white shirt would stand out like a beacon. He was doing everything he could to keep her hidden and make sure her shirt didn't alert their pursuers.

Another crack sounded, but it was farther away. The men searching for them must not have seen them and were moving off in another direction.

Her lungs screamed for air. Dark spots began to fill her vision. She could feel her energy seeping away. Her limbs went limp like noodles. A strange buzzing sounded in her ears. The weight lifted and everything turned on its axis.

"Jody."

She gasped, drawing a deep lungful of air, then another and another. The dark veil fell away. She blinked and looked up into Adam's beautiful eyes just inches from hers. His brow was lined with worry, his mouth tight as he gently shook her.

"Jody," he whispered harshly. "Are you okay?" He shook her again, his gaze searching hers.

She shoved his hands away. "I'm fine," she whispered. "Couldn't breathe."

He winced. "Sorry," he mouthed silently and held his fingers to his lips, letting her know they weren't alone, that the gunmen were still hunting them.

She pushed against his chest so she could get to her knees and follow wherever he led. Instead, he scooped her up into his arms and ran. He was bent over at the waist, keeping as low as possible so the bushes and trees could conceal them.

She clutched his shirt, holding on for dear life, the trees and bushes rushing past, making her dizzy. She squeezed her eyes shut and focused on making herself as small as possible, pulling in her arms and legs. It was a wild ride, with her bobbing up and down in his arms, feeling like she was going to fall any second. But he didn't let her fall. He protected her, as he'd done since the first moment he'd met her.

Where were the men who were after them? For him to be running like this, they must be close. But no one was shooting at them, so they must not have seen them. Not yet, anyway. She felt his chest rise and fall against hers. Carrying her and running in such an unnatural, bent-over position was taking its toll. His strides were slowing, his breaths coming faster and faster as he struggled to keep up his blistering pace.

"Put. Me. Down." Each word bounced out of her in unison with his strides.

Instead of stopping, he pulled her tighter against him, his mouth pressed next to her ear. "Too close," he rasped.

"I can run faster than you think. Put me down. *Please.*"

He stumbled and cursed, then stumbled again. He dropped to the ground, spilling her out of his arms onto a carpet of thick leaves and wild grasses. She scrambled to her knees and turned to check on him and ask which way they should run.

Then she froze.

She clasped her hand over her mouth to keep from crying out in dismay, mindful of the footfalls in the distance, pounding against the forest floor. Coming closer.

She scrambled to Adam, careful to stay low behind

the grasses and bushes. Tears stung the backs of her eyes as she met his pain-racked gaze. From midchest down, his body was wedged in some kind of hole, a sinkhole or maybe a wild animal's den. He'd braced his arms beside him and was struggling to pull himself free. But every time he moved, his face went pale. He was obviously in terrible pain.

Footfalls sounded harder against the ground, louder, coming closer.

Someone shouted. Another man answered, though Jody couldn't quite make out the words.

"Hide," Adam ordered, his voice low, gritty. Talking was obviously a struggle.

"I'm not leaving you in this hole," she whispered.

"Go." He pushed her hands away when she reached out to help him. He motioned toward the nearest stand of trees. "Hurry, before they see you."

Another shout sounded.

She reached for him again, but he shoved her hand away.

"Jody, get out of here. Head into those trees. There's nothing you can do to help me." He pressed his hands against the ground and strained, his arms shaking from the effort. His body barely moved. He was good and stuck.

She turned in a circle, desperate to find something that might help. There, a thick, broken piece of a branch a few feet away. She lunged for it, grabbed it and yanked it over to Adam. What now? There wasn't any room around his chest to shove the stick into the hole and try to pry him out.

"Over there," a shout sounded. "I think I saw something."

Adam grabbed her arm and yanked her close. "Leave me. Run into the woods. Save yourself, Jody. Hurry!"

"They'll kill you. I can't just hide while they find you and shoot you."

"There's no other choice. I'm stuck. Better that you survive than both of us die. *Go.*"

She whirled around again on her knees, looking for something else, anything, to give him a chance. There were boulders close by, but they wouldn't hide him for long. He was a sitting duck out here. Wait. Boulders. The branch she'd dragged over was too short, but if she got a longer one...

"Hold on," she whispered.

"Jody—"

She scrambled away from him, her heart pounding in rhythm with the footfalls she could hear. Taking a risk, she lifted up just enough to see over the closest bush, then ducked back down. All three men were in sight, about twenty feet apart from each other, maybe fifty yards away. They were searching behind every bush, every tree. They'd be here in a couple of minutes, maybe less. She turned around and around, then she saw it. Another branch, this one thicker, longer, like a bat or a thick cane. It would work. It had to.

She scrambled to it, then dragged it back to Adam and shoved both ends of the branch between some boulders. The main part of the branch was about a foot above him. He gave her a furious look, then grabbed the branch. It held. He strained against it, twisting and pulling. The ground around his chest moved. It was working.

"Did you hear something, Owen? Where did that come from?"

Adam froze and looked at Jody. "Go," he ordered again.

She hesitated.

He strained, pushing and pulling on the branch, twisting his body. He rose an inch, two, then fell back, his face a mirror of pain. The men were almost upon them. They would shoot him, kill him. Maybe they'd shoot her, too, wing her as he'd warned, take her prisoner so they could interrogate her for whatever they thought she had.

She glanced toward the trees where Adam had told her to run, to hide. The boulders and bushes might block her from sight long enough for her to reach cover. But that wouldn't save the honorable man caught in the hole, a man who'd risked his life repeatedly for her.

He was waving at her, his face a mask of fury as he tried to get her to run into the woods. She ignored him. She looked past the woods to the left. The trees were sparser there. But the ground was nearly level. A fast track, as her old high school coach would have said. And it wasn't close to Adam like the trees where he wanted her to hide.

She looked back at Adam, who looked like he wanted to murder her himself.

Please, please let this work. Let him live.

She bent over and ran in a crouch about thirty feet away from him. Then she stood.

"Over there!" Tattoo Guy yelled. "She's over there!"

Jody took off, arms and legs pumping as she sprinted across the open field.

Chapter Eight

Jody whirled around, swinging the knobby length of branch like a baseball bat when one of the men got too close.

The other two laughed as they continued to toy with her, slowly tightening their circle around her in the small clearing.

"What do you want from me?" she demanded.

The pockmarked one named Owen grinned and lunged toward her.

She swung the branch in a wide arc.

He jumped back, laughing and grinning the whole time. "She's feistier than her friend."

Her stomach dropped. "Where is she? Where's Tracy?" She tightened her grip on the branch, twisting and turning, trying to keep tabs on all three of them.

"She's alive," Tattoo Guy told her. "But she won't be for long if you don't tell me where your boss keeps all his pictures and videos."

She gritted her teeth. "Why don't you ask Sam?"

His mouth quirked in a cruel smile. "Already did. He

wasn't any more forthcoming than your little friend. I was hoping you'd be more cooperative."

"I told you. I don't know where any more pictures or videos are. Sam locks them all up in the office every day. Are you a client of his? Maybe you got things mixed up. Maybe you thought Sam had more information but he didn't—"

"Where's the cop, Jody girl?"

She clutched the branch harder. "He…he didn't make it. When we went over the cliff. I…had to leave his body there."

"Now, now, Jody." He stopped in front of her, just out of reach of her tree branch while the others kept circling. "And here I thought we were beginning to understand each other. But then you lie to me." He shook his head. "I don't like liars." He made a quick motion with his left hand.

Jody spun around in that direction, swinging her branch as hard and fast as she could. *Crack!* It slammed into the side of Owen's head. His eyes rolled up and he dropped to the ground, blood dribbling from the corner of his mouth.

She stared down at him in horror. Had she killed him? No, his chest moved. It moved again. He was breathing.

"Go on, Thad. Teach her a lesson."

She jerked her head up. Tattoo Guy was standing off to the side, still out of reach. The other man, Thad, was circling her again. But he wasn't smiling. And he was holding a knife.

She tightened her grip on the branch. Her heart was

beating so hard her pulse thudded in her ears. Had she really endured this whole horrible day only to die here, two hundred yards from where she'd left Adam? She hadn't managed to give him much distance to get away. Would he be able to escape before they backtracked and found him?

Thad darted toward her, knife extended.

She swung the branch.

He leaped back just in time, laughing again. He was enjoying this.

He feinted left, then jabbed toward her right.

She jumped to the side, bringing the branch around just in time to slap the knife back. That was close, too close. Her breaths came in short, choppy pants. They circled each other like two boxers. She tried to watch out for Tattoo Guy, keeping him in her peripheral vision. But Thad kept circling and she had to keep turning or risk him stabbing her from behind.

"We're wasting time, Thad. Just stick her already."

Jody's stomach clenched.

Thad's face scrunched up with concentration as he moved in for the kill. He raised the knife over his head, moved closer, closer.

She clutched the branch, knowing she might only get one chance.

Thad let out a guttural yell, a battle cry that made Jody's blood run cold. He lunged forward, knife raised. She screamed her fear, frustration and rage as she swung the branch with every ounce of strength she had.

"No!" Thad yelled, a split second before a dark shape barreled into him, slamming him to the ground.

Jody's swing met empty air. Her momentum sent her crashing to the ground, and the branch flew from her hand.

Vicious curses sounded from a few feet off to her left. Behind her came more swearing and thumps. She shoved herself up to her knees and looked around. Tattoo Guy was the one to her left, his face contorted in rage as he drew his gun. She jerked around to look behind her. Thad was on the ground, wrestling with the man who'd tackled him—Adam! And just a few feet away, the knife blade winked in the light, the prize Thad was struggling to grab.

Bam!

She ducked down and whirled around to see Tattoo Guy, gun out, pointing it at the two men locked in combat. He must have tried to shoot Adam. His jaw was clenched and the pistol kept moving in his two-handed grip as he waited for an opening between the fighting men on the ground.

Jody spun around and dived for the knife. Out of the corner of her eye, she saw Tattoo Guy turning toward her. She grabbed the hilt and threw the knife in one quick motion, twisting around and falling back onto the dirt.

A shout full of rage and pain filled the clearing. Tattoo Guy's pistol dropped to the ground. The knife's blade was buried in his left shoulder, blood quickly seeping around it and darkening his shirt. His eyes shined with malevolence and a promise of retribution as he stared at Jody. A shudder racked his body, and he dropped to his knees. His left arm hung useless at his side, but his right hand was already reaching for the pistol.

Scrambling away, Jody looked around for the only weapon she had, the branch.

Strong arms grabbed her from behind and yanked her backward. She struggled against them as she was picked up.

Tattoo Guy brought up his gun, shouting curses as he raised it.

She fell, something dark filling her vision as she slammed into the ground again.

Bam! Bam! Bam!

She recoiled against the sound of gunshots, but all she could see was the solid bulk of a downed tree directly in front of her face. She started to turn, but strong arms shoved her down—just like they'd done so many times before. Adam!

"Stay down," he whispered harshly.

More gunshots sounded. Wood splintered above her and rained down on her head.

Adam rose to his knees, beside her now, lifting a gun he must have taken from Thad and pointing it at the clearing. His return fire was deafening. Jody covered her ears, squeezing herself into a tight ball as more shots rang out.

A scuffling noise and more cursing sounded from a new direction. She could feel Adam's body against hers, pivoting to the right. He fired once, twice.

Bam! Another shot rang out from the left again.

Adam whirled around, cursing as he ducked behind the tree.

Footsteps pounded against the ground, the sound of men running away. The sounds faded, leaving only Adam's harsh breathing and her own shallow gasps to break the silence.

He looked down at her, gun still clenched in his hand. "They're gone. For now. Are you okay?"

She blinked up at him, noting the fresh blood on the side of his face, his hands, the white line of his lips, clenched in obvious pain. She uncurled and sat up, her gaze sweeping over him. His clothes were filthy and torn, matted with dirt and sweat. Then she saw it, finally, the reason he was in such terrible pain.

"Oh no." Her words clogged her suddenly tight throat as she stared in horror at the thick length of splintered wood that pierced his left calf, protruding through bloody holes torn in the front and back of his pant leg.

"Are you okay?" he repeated, his voice a gritty mixture of concern and raw pain.

"What? Yes, yes, I'm fine. But you, Adam, I can't even imagine how much that hurts." She reached for his left leg, but he jerked back.

"Leave it. We have to get moving. They'll lick their wounds, but they'll be back. It's not about whatever information you have anymore. It's about revenge. They'll kill both of us when they get the chance. We have to get out of here."

"But your leg. You can't possibly walk on that. You have to let me help you. I'll fashion a splint—"

"I made it this far. I can make it a little farther. We have to get to a defensible position. Hurry." He shoved the pistol into his front pocket then braced himself against the downed tree, pushing himself up.

Jody scrambled to her feet and stood beside him, reaching out to help him. Then she saw the body lying in the middle of the clearing. It wasn't Tattoo Guy or Owen. It was Thad. Sightless eyes stared up at the dark sky with its threatening storm that was still holding off, a single small dot of red in the center of his forehead. The ground beneath his head was saturated in blood.

She pressed a hand to her throat.

Adam's jaw worked, his hands clenched into fists at his sides. "That's the handiwork of our nemesis, Tattoo Guy. My guess is he didn't want to leave anyone behind who might give us information about him."

Her gaze flew to his. "He killed his own man?"

He nodded. "Which means he won't hesitate to kill us, especially since you managed to hit him with that knife. He doesn't strike me as the forgive-and-forget type. As soon as he binds his wound and is able to come after us again, he will. And it wouldn't surprise me if he brings reinforcements. We have to get out of here, fall back to somewhere more secure, keep moving until we get in range of a cell tower and can radio for help."

He wobbled on his feet, then braced himself against the tree.

She bit her lip to keep from crying out in sympathy. He was being unbelievably strong, had managed to somehow crawl out of that hole where she'd left him. And even with his leg so horribly damaged, he'd come to her rescue. Somehow she had to find the inner strength to match his, so she could get him somewhere safe and finally look in his backpack for a first-aid kit. Her mouth twisted bitterly. He needed far more than a kit. He needed an emergency room with a trauma unit.

"Let's go. That way." He pointed off toward the left.

"Deeper into the mountains? Are you sure? Shouldn't we head back toward town—"

He shook his head. "Our only real chance is to get in range of a cell tower so I can radio for a rescue team. Back the way we came is by the broken tower, the one destroyed in the wildfires. If we head west, we should be in range of a working tower within a few minutes."

"A few minutes?"

"Give or take."

Relief made her legs go weak. Soon they would have other rangers with guns to protect them, and medical help for Adam. And then they could bring in the FBI or whoever they needed in order to find her friend Tracy. And Sam, if he was still alive. Then they could put Tattoo Guy and Owen in prison where they belonged.

Maybe, just maybe, they'd make it out of here after all.

Adam turned and limped forward.

"Wait." She motioned for him to stay where he was and hurried around the downed tree.

"Jody, what are you—"

"This." She held up the thick piece of branch she'd used like a bat to defend herself after the thugs had caught up to her and surrounded her. "It's thick and heavy and just about long enough to work as a cane." She rushed over to him and held it out.

The lines of pain bracketing his mouth eased, and

he offered her a small smile. "That should do the job. Thanks. The one I used to pull myself out of the hole broke in half or it would have been a perfect walking stick." He tested it out, pressing the length of branch against the ground as he took a step forward. He grimaced but quickly smoothed his features. "Works great. Let's go."

Together they hobbled and walked west, keeping near the tree line to give them cover in case the bad guys came looking for them. By staying out of the woods, the going was easier, with fewer obstacles for Adam to navigate around.

"Shouldn't we stop and pull that wood out of your leg?"

He shook his head. "It's controlling the bleeding. It's better to leave it in, even though it hurts like the devil."

She nodded, unconvinced. But since her most recent medical training was CPR in the fifth grade, it wasn't like she had any true wisdom to offer.

"At least the storm is holding off. That's good," she said.

He looked up and nodded. "Looks like it's moving east. We should be okay."

At first, he managed a steady clip. But as they began a gradual climb into the foothills of the next mountain, his pace began to lag. He was leaning heavier and heavier on the makeshift cane. If the broken piece of wood piercing his leg was truly stanching the bleeding, she couldn't imagine how bad it would be if the wood was out. A dark, wet spot was slowly spreading down his pant leg.

She glanced at the ground behind him. Bright spots of blood marked their trail. She worried her bottom lip, not sure whether it mattered at this point. They weren't going fast enough to outrun anyone. Once the bad guys decided to come back to look for them, they'd find them pretty quickly, with or without a blood trail to follow.

"What is it?" Adam asked, his voice husky from the pain.

"Nothing."

He stopped, using the cane for support as he drew a ragged breath. "It's not nothing. What's wrong?"

"It's just that, well, we're leaving a pretty obvious trail. I doubt it matters, but—"

He glanced back, then swore. "My backpack. There should be an extra shirt inside. We can wrap it—"

"I'm on it." She moved behind him and quickly located the shirt, then zipped the pack. A moment later, she stepped back to take a look. The shirt had been wrapped tight around his leg, just under where the stick protruded. It was soaking up the blood and had the added advantage of stabilizing the stick. There'd been some white-lipped moments as he'd endured her ministrations. "That should do the trick," she said. "Hopefully it will help ease the pain a bit when you walk, too."

He took a step forward then another. No blood was left on the ground behind him. But his white-knuckled grip on the makeshift cane told her the pain, if anything, was worse.

They had to get him help. Soon.

"Do you think we're in range of a tower yet?" She moved to his side, wedging her shoulder beneath his to help him hobble forward. It was a testament to his agony that he didn't refuse her help like he'd done earlier.

"Let's give it a few more minutes before we try," he said. "I can picture the park map in my head. I think once we get right about to that tree over there—" he waved toward a group of trees about a football field's length away "—that should do it."

As they hobbled toward their goal, she said, "I never thanked you for saving me in the clearing. I don't know how you managed it. But I was a goner until you got there. Thank you."

"Don't thank me. I'm just doing—"

"Your job, yes, I know. But I guarantee most people wouldn't go to the lengths you've gone to in order to help a stranger. So maybe instead of arguing with me when I thank you, you can just say 'you're welcome.'"

His mouth twitched but didn't quite manage to form a smile. "You're welcome."

She squeezed his side in response, and they continued forward.

An eternity seemed to pass before they reached the trees he'd pointed to. She helped him turn around and sit on some rocks.

He let out a shaky breath and gave her a reassuring smile. "It's going to be okay, Jody. We're going to make it."

"No offense," she said, "but once your fellow rangers finally get here and get us off these mountains, I'm never planning on coming back again. I've had my fill of the Great Smoky Mountains National Park."

He chuckled and unsnapped his radio from his utility belt. Then he lifted it and froze.

Jody swung around, looking behind them. But she didn't see anyone. Or hear anyone. As far as she could tell, they were alone. "What's wrong?" She turned back around to see him staring off into space, a defeated expression on his face. "Adam?"

Without a word, he held up the radio. A bullet hole had been blasted right through the screen.

Chapter Nine

Jody stared at the bullet hole. "Maybe…maybe the radio will work anyway."

He turned some dials. "It's busted. Useless."

"But—"

"Forget it." He snapped the radio back onto his belt and looked past her, his gaze scanning the horizon. "I figure Tattoo Guy will get that shoulder stitched up and some painkillers on board before he and reinforcements come after us. As fast as he got that third guy out here—"

"Thad."

He nodded. "Thad. As fast he got him out here, he's probably got more resources close by. It won't take long." He pulled Thad's pistol out of his holster and popped out the magazine. Then he popped it back in and shoved the gun into the holster. "Six shots left in the magazine and one in the chamber. It's a .40 caliber, like my Glock was. So the extra magazines in my backpack will work. We won't be completely defenseless. We'll need to find a defensible position and settle in, make a plan."

"A plan sounds good. What's our first move?"

He shrugged the backpack off his shoulders and let it drop to the ground. "That first aid kit you've been nagging me about?"

"I don't nag."

He winked, which was amazing considering that he had a piece of wood sticking through his leg.

"The kit is in the bottom of the pack. Can you get it for me?"

"Of course." She dropped to her knees, grimacing when the cuts and scrapes on her skin started stinging all over again. She rummaged through the pack, noting he had some water and energy bars, which would come in handy when they weren't busy running for their lives. She grabbed one of the bottles and handed it to him. "Drink that."

"Not yet." He set the unopened bottle on top of the rock.

She pulled the medical kit out and handed it to him. "You need to hydrate to help your body fight its injuries and replenish the blood you've lost. Why won't you drink now?"

"Because there's something else we need to do first."

He clicked the top of the plastic box open, rummaged inside, then pulled out a spool of black thread and a long, wicked-looking needle.

"If we're going to face off with our enemies," he said, "I can't afford to lose any more blood. And I need to be mobile. I'm going to pull the stick out of my leg. And you're going to stitch me up."

ADAM WOULD HAVE sworn Jody's face turned green when he asked her to sew him up. Now it was completely washed out, almost translucent. Her right hand went to her stomach.

"St...stitch you up?"

"It's a lot to expect," he said. "And I hate asking it of you. But once I pull out the wood, I'll be bleeding from the front and back of my leg. It's going to take both of us to stanch the bleeding and sew the wounds closed."

She shook her head, stepping back from him. "I threw up earlier just because I was upset. Sticking a needle in someone's flesh is a whole other level. I can't do it."

"You can. You're much stronger than you think you are. How many people do you know who could have taken off like you did, leading the bad guys away from me? You saved my life, Jody. You know it. And then you faced down three men with guns and knives and lived to tell the tale. You're a hero and a fighter. You *can* do this."

Her shoulders straightened as his words sank in. Some of the color came back to her cheeks. Then she glanced down at the needle and thread and went pale again. "Please tell me you have anesthesia to numb the pain."

He slowly shook his head. "No. I don't."

"Alcohol?"

"The drinking kind or the rubbing kind?" he teased.

"Either! You have to have something for the pain, and germs."

"Afraid I'm all out of whiskey. But I do have an antiseptic spray. And rolls of gauze."

She raised a shaky hand to her throat. "It will hurt like crazy."

"It already hurts like crazy. Nothing you do could make it worse." He leaned forward and took her hand in his. "I need your help. We're sitting ducks out here. Not enough cover. I'd keep going, look for somewhere better to do this if I could. But in case you hadn't noticed, that shirt you wrapped around my leg is soaked through already. We're leaving a blood trail again. And I'm getting woozy. We have to stop the bleeding, now, or I won't be any use to you at all. I won't be able to defend you. I'll be passed out."

"I'm so sorry," she whispered.

He frowned, thinking she was still refusing to work on his leg. But then she took the thread and needle from him and dropped to her knees. She was probably apologizing because she didn't want to hurt him. He didn't think he'd ever met anyone more sensitive and kindhearted than her.

She set the first-aid kit beside her and located the antiseptic spray. He stretched his leg out in front of him to give her better access. She used his knife to slit his pants and roll the ends up to his knee, out of the way.

Once Jody Ingram set her mind on something, she fully committed to it. She was like a drill sergeant, giving him orders, setting out what she needed.

Getting his boot off to give her more room to stitch the wound was agony. But it was over quickly.

Another of his shirts, the only other one he had in

the pack, was sacrificed for the cause. She wrapped it around his calf just below the entry and exit points of the piece of wood, ready to apply pressure as soon as the wood came out.

The confidence she'd displayed as she prepared his leg seemed to evaporate when she looked up at him with shiny eyes. "I'm going to do this," she assured him. "But I'm probably going to cry the whole time and I might even throw up. You'll just have to deal with it, all right?"

He was surprised that she could make him laugh when he was in so much pain. "All right."

She nodded. "Go ahead, then. I'm ready. Pull it out." She squeezed her eyes shut and braced his calf.

In spite of the pain—and the even more pain that was yet to come—he couldn't help but smile at her and admire her. He'd meant what he said. She really was courageous, heroic and strong. She was also sensitive and kind, a rare combination these days.

He crossed his ankles, using his good leg as a brace to keep his other leg still. Then he grasped the two-inch-thick length of tree branch that had impaled him when he'd slid into the pit. His calf already throbbed just from grasping the wood. This was going to hurt like the dickens. And he had to be quiet, no matter how much it hurt, so he wouldn't upset Jody any more than she already was. And so he didn't broadcast their location to the thugs in case they were already back in the mountains looking for them.

He mentally counted. One. Two. Three. He locked his good leg down hard on the bad one, and pulled. The pain was instantaneous, blinding in its intensity, molten lava searing every nerve ending. There was a sickening sucking sound as he tugged and pulled the stick forward and up. It slid through his leg, scraping against bone, rough bumps on the wood tearing his flesh anew much like an arrow might have done. It finally came free with a popping sound.

Jody gasped and clamped her hands down hard against his leg to stop the fresh rush of blood.

Agony ripped through him. He had to clench his jaw not to yell. His lungs heaved. Sweat poured off him. He gasped for air, quick pants as he tried to breathe through the pain.

"It's bleeding too much. I can't stop it."

Her words came to him through a long black tunnel. He struggled against it, desperately tried to clear his vision.

"Adam? Adam!"

He surrendered to the darkness.

JODY'S HAND SHOOK so hard that she almost couldn't sew the last stitch. Only the fact that it was the very last one kept her going. Because she knew it would soon be over. Her stomach clenched as she pierced Adam's skin and pulled the last of his ragged flesh together. She shuddered as she used the knife to cut the thread.

He was still unconscious. But his chest rose and fell in steady, deep breaths. And she'd checked his pulse about ten times out of fear. It too was strong and steady. Maybe the universe was being kind to him by knocking him out so he wouldn't experience the pain of being stitched up. She'd barely managed to keep him from knocking his head when he'd fallen back. But she hadn't been able to keep him from sliding off the boulder.

Now he was lying on his side on the ground, which had ended up being easier for her to stitch the wounds. But without him awake to help her put pressure on them while she stitched them up, he'd lost far more blood than he could probably afford. And she'd had to work fast to try to limit the bleeding. There'd been absolutely no finesse in her needlework. He was going to have horrible scars.

She bent over his leg, inspecting her work, and winced. Hopefully men didn't care about such things. Or maybe a plastic surgeon could fix it later. She glanced around. If there *was* a later. He was right about them being out in the open here. It was called a bald, if she remembered right from the brochures she'd seen. A part of the mountains where there was a huge gap in the trees, where nothing but grass grew. It could have been caused by disease, but judging by the charring on the few trees that were close by, more likely it was a part of the woods that had burned all the way to the ground, leaving nothing in its wake.

And nothing but a few rocks and trees to hide behind.

She grabbed a bottle of water and a bandana from the backpack and gently wiped away the blood on his leg. Thankfully, the stitches had done their job. The bleeding had stopped. Her next worry was infection. She'd sprayed the disinfectant on it throughout the process. And she sprayed it liberally one more time before carefully rolling gauze around his calf.

Once that was done, she pulled a clean sock up over the wound to help protect it. After another quick check to make sure he was still breathing, she worked his boot back on. She almost gave up, but knowing it would probably hurt like crazy if he was awake for the procedure, she persevered until the boot was in place.

She put everything into one of the baggies in his backpack, remembering the "take nothing, leave nothing" mantra the commercials were always touting to tourists. Then she sat beside him and wondered what to do next. Shouldn't he have woken up by now? She pressed the back of her hand to his forehead. It seemed normal, as far as she could tell. No sign of fever. Not yet, anyway. So why wasn't he waking up?

She shook his shoulders. "Adam, it's Jody. Adam, can you hear me?" She shook him again, then sat back and looked around. There were a few trees close by, and the group of boulders he was lying beside. But it wasn't enough to make her feel safe by any means. And she hated for him to be so vulnerable. Maybe she could pull him behind the boulders at least? It would block anyone's view from the woods back where they'd emerged when running from Tattoo Guy. It was worth a try.

A few minutes later, she gave up. A five-foot featherweight like her just wasn't going to be able to drag tall, dark and gorgeous anywhere. It was hopeless. She thought about trying to roll him, but she was worried she'd hurt his leg. There was only one other thing she could think to do—guard him. She pulled the pistol out of his pocket. It was a Ruger, not a brand she'd ever owned or shot before. But it was similar to the Glock she had in the safe at her apartment. It was small enough to fit comfortably in her hand.

After unloading it, she dry fired it a few times. Not the best thing for the gun. But she wanted to be familiar with the trigger pull, see how hard she had to squeeze to make it shoot. It was a little trickier than her own gun, but not overly difficult.

She loaded it again and dug the two extra magazines of ammo from the bottom of the backpack and put them in her pocket. Then she scooted her back against the boulder beside Adam's unconscious form.

Clutching the pistol with both hands, she rested it in her lap, sitting cross-legged on the ground. Then she stared toward the woods, and waited.

Chapter Ten

Blinding, sharp pain shot through Adam's body. He jerked upright, clawing for the pistol holstered on his belt. It wasn't there. He shoved his hands in his pockets, desperately searching for his weapon.

"Whoa, whoa, Adam, stop. You're okay. Everything's okay."

His hands clutched nothing but emptiness in his pockets. He blinked in confusion at the beautiful woman kneeling in front of him. Thick red hair formed a messy, wavy halo around her heart-shaped face, falling to just below her shoulders. Her blouse was partly undone, revealing a lacy bra and the delicious upper curves of her breasts. His mouth watered as his gaze traveled to her full, pink lips, which were curved in a smile as she leaned close.

"Sorry for thumping your leg. You'd slept so long. I was getting worried and thought that might be the only way to wake you up. Looks like it worked." She smiled sheepishly, then her smile faded. "Adam? It's me. Jody. Don't you recognize me?"

He watched her lips move like a blind man seeking the light.

She put her hand on his shoulder and leaned in closer. "Adam?"

It was all the invitation he needed. He wrapped one arm around her waist, sank the other deep into her fall of gorgeous red hair and pulled her mouth to his. Her lips parted on a gasp, and he groaned, tasting their honeyed sweetness and delving deeper inside.

She was so hot and sweet and soft. He tasted and treasured her mouth, ran his hand down her back, down the sexy curve of her bottom, wanting her with a desperation that didn't make sense. Nothing made sense. He didn't know how he'd gotten here or why this woman—Jody—was in his bed. But he wasn't going to complain or waste the opportunity.

She moaned deep in her throat and clutched his shoulders. Then, finally, she was kissing him back. For such a tiny thing, she was full of passion and exploded like a firecracker in his arms. Her breasts crushed against his chest, and she threaded her hands through his hair, her tongue dueling with his.

He shuddered and caressed her through her shorts. She jerked against him. For a moment he thought she might push him away. But then she was kissing him again. His body hardened painfully. He couldn't take this much longer. He had to have her. Now. He slid his hands back to her blouse and fumbled with the buttons. She was too close. His big hands couldn't maneuver between them and he was afraid he'd rip the fabric.

He broke the kiss and drew a ragged breath as he

gently pushed her back so he could finish taking off her shirt. Deep green eyes stared back at him in wonder over green-framed glasses perched crookedly on her nose. A delightful smattering of freckles marched across her flushed cheeks as her gaze dropped to his lips. He undid one button, then another, then he stopped.

A pistol lay discarded on the ground between them, cradled between her thighs. He frowned. That wasn't his pistol. He looked at his utility belt and saw the radio, its cracked screen glinting in the fading light. Fading light? He leaned back and looked around. Little puffs of white mist dotted the mountains all around them, looking like signals from some Indian campfire of old. The Smoky Mountains. They were outside, in the middle of the Smokies. And the sun was going down?

He made a more careful inspection of their surroundings, noting they were out in the open, in a bald near the foothills. His legs were stretched out in front of him. His lap was full of gorgeous redhead. And his left leg was shooting hot jolts of lava up his calf. He winced and bent to the side to see why it hurt. White gauze was wrapped around it just above where his boot ended. The whole lower part of his pants was gone, the hem ragged and ripped, like someone had torn it, or sawed it with a serrated knife.

"Adam?" Her husky voice made his body jerk in response, blood heating his veins, scorching him from the inside out. Good grief, this woman was sexy. He drew a deep breath and turned back toward her.

And blinked.

Recognition slammed into him. Everything clicked

together. The hazy fog of lust cleared instantly, and his mouth dropped open in shock. "Jody?"

Her perfectly shaped brows arched in confusion. "Adam? Why are you…" Her eyes widened, a look of horror crossing her face. "You didn't know it was me?"

He stared at her, his face flushing with guilty heat. "I…I knew there was a beautiful woman—"

She scrambled off his lap, smooth toned arms and glorious legs flailing awkwardly in her rush to get away from him. One of her legs slammed into his left calf. Fire ripped through his body. He sucked in a breath and jerked back, clenching his jaw to keep from shouting.

"Oh no, your leg. I'm so sorry. So, so sorry."

She reached for him, but he shook his head and held a hand up to stop her. "Don't." His voice was a harsh croak, the pain so intense he couldn't say anything else. He drew several deep breaths, holding as still as possible, waiting, hoping the pain would ease its grip.

"I'm sorry," she whispered miserably, her eyes looking suspiciously bright, like she was holding back tears.

On a scale of one to ten, his pain was about fifty-two. He rode it out, his fingers clawing at the dirt, panting like a wounded animal. Darkness wavered at the edges of his vision. But he couldn't give in. He realized he must have passed out before, when he'd pulled out the piece of wood embedded in his leg. Thankfully, their pursuers hadn't come back yet or they'd be dead. Or maybe not. As the pain began to ease to about a thirty, he noted Jody had grabbed the gun, expertly holding it with her finger on the frame, not the trigger, pointing it away from him.

"You've…" He cleared his gritty throat and tried again. "You've fired guns before. You know how…how to handle them."

He tried to focus on her rather than the pain. Had he noticed how beautiful her hair was before? It was fire red and hung in thick waves past her shoulders.

She looked down at the pistol in her hand and frowned. "Well, yes. Of course I know how to handle guns. Once I left home and went to college, I was determined to never be a victim again, so I…" Her eyes widened, as if she'd just realized what she'd let slip. "I mean, that I would never *become* a victim, so I learned about guns and—"

"Jody? Who hurt you?"

She looked away. "I never said anyone hurt me."

"You mentioned your family before, that you weren't close. Did one of them—"

"I'm really sorry about your leg," she blurted out, obviously desperate to change the subject. "Is it feeling any better? I didn't mean to bump it. I'm so sorry."

"Stop." The fire in his left leg was bearable now, a paltry eleven or twelve. He let out a shuddering breath. "Stop apologizing all the time. All the bad in the world isn't your fault or your responsibility. Okay?"

She nodded but didn't look like she believed him. "I didn't mean to hit your leg just then. Earlier I did— just a tiny nudge, though. I was worried about you and wanted to wake you…" Her voice trailed off, and her gaze fell to his lips. Her pink tongue darted out to moisten her mouth.

His entire body clenched. He forced himself to look

away from the tempting little siren. And just how had that happened anyway? How had she gone from being the young, barely-out-of-college girl to a sexy, mature woman who could tempt a saint? He must have a fever. That was it. It was the only explanation. Jody was far too pure and innocent and sweet for a jaded man like him.

"Make me laugh."

She blinked. "What?"

"Make me laugh. Say something funny." When she continued to look blankly at him, he said, "The pain, to take my mind off the pain. Tell me something funny." What he really needed to do was take his mind off how sexy she was. He clenched his hands into fists to keep from reaching for her.

Her brow furrowed in concentration, as if he'd asked her to calculate some complex scientific equation instead of trying to come up with a lame joke. Didn't she ever laugh? Or really smile and have fun? He found himself craving her smile and laughter even more than he craved her body.

And that was saying something.

"Peter, Patricia, Patience, Patrick and Paul," she blurted out.

He waited for the punch line. "Picked a peck of pickled peppers?"

She frowned. "No. The names. Peter, Patricia, Patience, Patrick and Paul. Those are the names of my adoptive father and my adoptive sisters and brothers."

"Wait, seriously?"

She nodded, looking even more serious than she had a few moments earlier.

"What's your adoptive mother's name? Penelope?"

She shook her head. "Her name is Amelia."

Adam threw his head back and laughed. He laughed so hard he got a stitch in his side. Then Jody had to ruin it by smiling, a genuine, real smile that reached her gorgeous green eyes and made her so beautiful he ached. Again. Oh, how he wanted her, needed her. He sobered and stared at her, his breath hitching when he noticed the tantalizing display she obviously wasn't aware that she was offering. "Jody. Your blouse is, ah, gaping a bit."

She didn't even look down at her shirt. "So?"

His mouth was watering, just from that one glimpse of heaven he'd had, before he'd forced himself to look up, at her face. She obviously hadn't understood what he was trying to tell her. "I can see…ah…your…your bra is…showing."

"In case you didn't notice, I was letting you unbutton my blouse earlier. I'm well aware of the state of my clothes. You may have temporarily lost your mind, forgetting who I was. But I didn't. And I'm not ashamed of that. You're a gorgeous guy. And I like you, a lot. Okay, a whole lot. I wouldn't mind picking up where we left off."

His mouth fell open. He snapped it closed.

"What?" She sounded angry this time, on top of being frustrated. "Does that shock you?"

He cleared his throat. "Well, yes, actually, it does. A little. You're so, so…"

Her eyes narrowed. "I'm so what?"

"Young," he blurted out.

Her expression changed to one of confusion. "I'm twenty-four. Yes, I'm young. But I'm not *that* young. I'm a full-grown woman, Adam. Not some child. Where on earth did you get this hang-up about women who are younger than you?"

He scrubbed the stubble on his face, wondering just how this conversation had turned so bizarre. "You're right." He dropped his hands to his sides. "When we met, I got it in my head that you were much younger than you are, and I didn't for a second imagine ever, well, being attracted to you."

She stiffened.

"Oh, come on," he said. "Don't get insulted now. There can't be any doubt about the state of my attraction for you at this point." He waved at his overly tight pants and his still-painful erection. "I think we crossed that barrier about the time you stuck your tongue down my throat."

She made a choking sound, her eyes wide. She coughed, then covered her mouth with her hands. He had the crazy suspicion that she was laughing at him and didn't want him to know. Likely she was trying to spare his feelings. Because that would be typical for someone who felt guilty over everything from global warming to La Niña and everything else she had no control over.

"I want you, okay?" he gritted out. "And the age thing isn't the problem anymore. The problem, if there is one, is that you're too nice."

Her hand fell to her lap. "I'm too nice? What's that supposed to mean?"

"It means you're too pure, too sweet, too…nice. You deserve someone way better than me. I'd destroy everything good about you. I'd destroy you. You don't want me."

"I don't?" She sounded suspiciously like she wanted to laugh again. "Because you'll ruin me? That's a bit old-fashioned of you. Besides, I'm not a virgin, Adam."

Something dark passed in her eyes, but it was gone too quickly for him to be sure what he'd seen. Pain? Anger? Resentment? At who? Him, or someone in her past?

"Jody, I'm sorry if I offended you, or hurt you. I didn't—"

"Stop apologizing." She parroted his earlier words back at him. "It's not like I was asking for a long-term commitment." She pulled the edges of her blouse together. "We were just two adults who were about to have fun." She looked wistfully at his lap. "A *lot* of fun. But the moment has passed. And I think that ship has definitely sailed."

His hands curled against his thighs. It was either that or grab her and prove that the ship had definitely *not* sailed. This ridiculous conversation had only done one thing to his appetite for her—whet it.

She pushed herself up and wiped dirt off her legs before straightening. "I need a moment of privacy. When I come back, we'll work on a plan to get out of here and back to civilization."

What should have been a dramatic exit when she

whirled around to leave was ruined when she tripped on a tree root. Her arms cartwheeled and she managed to regain her balance without falling. Her spine snapped ramrod straight and her face was flaming red when she once again turned her back on him and marched off to the nearest stand of trees.

Adam groaned and dropped his head to his chest. Everything about this day, from the moment he'd stepped on the Sugarland Mountain Trail, was a disaster. And every attempt he made to fix it only seemed to make things worse.

He shook his head. He wouldn't let anything happen to the complicated, intriguing, sexy redhead who'd just declared that she was no longer interested in him. It was just as well. Because he needed to focus, to figure out a plan. They needed to alert someone about Tracy, get them searching for her. Which meant he needed to be fully mobile and find that defensible position he'd mentioned earlier.

Even if they didn't find a way out of the mountains to get help, he knew his team would come looking for him soon, if they weren't already. The sun had slipped low on the horizon, and night was falling. His shift had ended hours ago and he'd never called in to report status updates.

His truck was still parked in the employee lot behind the visitor's center. It wasn't like he worked in an office building. He worked in the wilderness. No one would just assume that if he didn't show up he'd gone bar-hopping with a friend to drink away his Saturday night. They had each other's backs and took it seriously when a member of the team didn't report in. But there were thousands of acres of mountain range out here. Without a last known location, they could have several teams of search and rescue out here and never find him.

It had happened before.

Two different people on separate occasions had disappeared in the Smoky Mountains National Park over the past couple of years. They were never found. Not alive, anyway. What Adam had to do was figure out a way to improve their odds, to help the searchers find them. Or reach the searchers themselves.

Which meant he had to stand up.

He also needed a few moments of privacy, like Jody. His bladder was near to bursting. Which meant he *really* needed to stand up. And walk. Neither option appealed to him with his leg throbbing painfully in rhythm with his heartbeat. He had no desire to experience the agony he'd felt when he'd pulled the stick free from his leg, or when Jody had accidentally kicked his leg while scrambling off his lap. But there was no getting around it. He was destined for a bit of torture no matter what. Might as well get it over with. Of course, deciding that he needed to get up and figuring out how to do it were two entirely different problems.

His burning, aching leg wouldn't support him enough to rise to standing. Even rolling over on all fours failed. The leg was pretty much useless. He was beginning to wonder about the wisdom of having pulled out the stick. It had seemed like the only way to stop the bleeding. But his muscles were like jelly now, unable to bear up under any kind of strain.

After yet another try, he got halfway up before his leg collapsed beneath him and he fell face-first into the dirt. He cursed viciously and rolled to his side, panting like a dog as he fought through yet another episode of stabbing pain that set his insides on fire.

When the pain finally subsided to a dull roar rather than a blistering inferno, he stared toward the trees they'd come from several hours ago. The sun had set. The moon was bright, the sky clear, or he wouldn't have been able to see anything this far away from any man-made light sources. Still, the woods were little more than a dark void.

Had Tattoo Guy given up on coming after them? Figuring they'd die of exposure out here? Or was he biding his time, waiting to see where Jody was before shooting at Adam?

Jody. He looked to his right where she'd disappeared earlier. How long had she been gone? More than five minutes, which was all it should have taken her if she had to empty her bladder. Had it been ten minutes? Fifteen?

He hated himself for having spent so much energy and time on his repeated attempts to stand. He had no true concept of the passage of time. And no clue whether she was in trouble, or admiring the stars, or walking off her anger at him and how badly he'd bungled things between them. Regardless, she should have been back by now. He *had* to get up and go check on her. There was no other option.

He looked around, searching for something to use as leverage. The makeshift walking stick might have helped. But the tall grasses and rocks dotting the landscape were hiding it well and good. Wait, rocks. They'd stopped by some boulders to work on his leg. He'd been sitting on one before he'd passed out. He jerked around and let out a string of curses when he realized the boulder had been behind him this whole time. Bracing his arms on either side of him, he scooted back until he was against the rock. Then he rolled over, breathing through the worst of the pain before bracing his hands on the boulder.

With his good leg beneath him and his hands pushing against the rock, he finally made it to his feet. Correction, foot. His bad leg crumpled as soon as he put weight on it. He had to balance on one foot to keep from falling. Leaning against the boulder to remain upright, he looked toward the small group of trees again for Jody. No sign of her. Where was she? At least she had his gun for protection.

Or did she?

He looked around, then groaned. The gun was lying on the ground by the boulder. She hadn't taken it. He swiped it and checked the loading, then slid it into his pocket. Where was his walking stick? He didn't see it anywhere. He snagged his backpack, too, and clipped the strap across his chest to keep it in place so it wouldn't fall with him hopping around like a kangaroo.

On a hunch, he continued his kangaroo impression around the boulder to the back side. *Yes*. The walking stick was lying there, probably having fallen when he'd sat down. He grabbed it and tested it out.

At first his leg wobbled so much he could barely take a step. But he did take a step, so he was encouraged by that. He took another then another. After about ten feet, the leg began to go numb. Probably not a good sign. But it made walking more bearable. And faster. He hurried as quickly as he could across the open space from the boulder to the trees. Then he stopped. Beyond the trees was more empty space.

And no sign of Jody.

"Jody," he called out, his voice just above a whisper. A cool mountain breeze ruffled his hair, bringing with it the scent of rain. The storm that had threatened earlier seemed to be brewing again instead of moving off to the east as he'd expected. "Jody," he called out, louder this time. The only answer he heard was the distant rumble of thunder. A flash of lightning followed, off to the left.

He took another step past the trees and looked around in a full circle for something, anything, that might tell him where she'd wandered off to. Thunder rumbled again, followed by another flash of light. But this time the light didn't turn off. It kept coming. Toward him, low to the ground. That wasn't lightning. And the sound he'd heard wasn't thunder.

It was an ATV, its engine making a dull roar now, the headlights bouncing crazily as it rushed toward him.

He dived for the cover of trees, pulling himself behind them just as the headlights swept past where he'd been standing moments ago.

The ATV wasn't an ATV after all. It was a dune buggy. Tattoo Guy was driving. Owen and another man were in the back seat, Owen with a rifle in his hand, pointed up at the sky. And in the front, her eyes wide with terror, her hands tied to the roll bar above her, was Jody.

Chapter Eleven

Jody bit her lip to keep from shouting a warning to Adam as the buggy bounced across the bald and headed toward the group of rocks and boulders where she'd seen him last. She could only hope that he'd heard the engine, seen the headlights and been able to hobble to another hiding place in time. If he was just crouching down behind the boulder, the men would see him in about, three, two, one...he wasn't there. Her breath stuttered out in relief.

The backpack was gone, too. And the gun.

The buggy continued on its way, circling the area as the men looked for Adam. He was injured. He was also experienced and trained. He would know what to do, wouldn't he? He'd mentioned earlier getting to a more defensible position. Had he done that now? She hoped so. Because there was no doubt what the men with her would do if they found him.

They'd kill him.

"He ain't here, Damien," Owen called out.

Tattoo Guy—now she knew his name was Damien—aimed a sour look at Owen in the rearview mirror. "Unless he sprouted wings, he's here. You saw that stick through his leg in the clearing. He won't be running any marathons any time soon. He's hiding. We just have to find him."

He slammed his foot on the brake, wincing when the action obviously jostled his hurt shoulder. His left arm was in a sling. Adam had been right. He'd had resources close by and got medical treatment, then returned with reinforcements—including the man whom Owen had called Ned, sitting quietly in the back seat studying the terrain, and four more men in a second buggy that was searching the other side of the bald.

The buggy slid to a stop, its headlights illuminating the boulder where she and Adam had been earlier—before she'd gone into the woods to relieve her bladder. It was a mixed blessing that she'd chosen not to stop at the first stand of trees. Because when Tattoo Guy, Damien, had found her, she'd been far away from Adam. And that was the only reason he was still alive.

She'd wanted more privacy, which seemed silly given how intimate they'd already been. Still, it had been good luck that she'd continued on. And that after she'd answered nature's call, she'd seen a beautiful stream sparkling in the moonlight in the distance. She'd been unable to quell the artistic excitement inside her that wanted to see nature's beauty. As soon as she'd stepped up to the stream, Damien had grabbed her.

The radio sitting on the console crackled to life. He picked it up and spoke to his other team, comparing notes about where they'd searched.

Jody rubbed her tongue against the inside of her sore

cheek, trying to ease the ache where he'd punched her when she'd refused to tell him where "the cop" was. She imagined the only reason he hadn't beaten her more was that he figured Adam was close by and they'd find him quickly. Since that hadn't happened, would he hit her again?

He slammed the radio back into the console. "Where's the cop?" He called her a foul name and raised his fist in warning. "Where is he?"

She backed against the door. "I don't know. I told you, we split up after the clearing. We were trying to find a cabin, or a road, and I got lost. I couldn't figure out how to get back to where we'd agreed to rendezvous."

"She's probably telling the truth," Owen offered from the back seat. "You know how redheads are."

Damien frowned and glanced back at him. "Don't you mean blondes?"

"Oh, yeah. Those, too. See?"

Damien closed his eyes and shook his head, then looked at Jody again. "Where was the rendezvous point?"

Keep it simple, stupid. The KISS principle one of her criminal justice professors had badgered them with every time they came up with some convoluted answer to a question came to her rescue now. There was evidence by that boulder—blood on the ground, footprints—that would corroborate her story without giving up Adam's current location, wherever that happened to be.

"There!" She poured excitement into her voice. "That boulder, see? I remember it now. I'm sure there have to be some footprints or something showing you we were there." She bit her lip. "At least, I think that's the right boulder."

He stared at her a long moment, apparently not nearly as willing as his pal Owen to believe she was a "dumb redhead."

"Check it out," Damien ordered, waving toward the boulder.

Owen popped his door open.

"Not you," Damien said. "Ned. See what you can find."

With a barely perceptible nod, the second man hopped over the door frame and landed nimbly on the ground. He produced a pen-size flashlight from one of his pockets and shined it around the base of the boulder. As Jody watched, he crouched down and feathered his fingers over some depressions in the grass.

He shined the light all around, his intense gaze seeming to take everything in, as if he could picture what had happened there. Then he aimed his flashlight farther out, toward the trees where she'd run earlier. He stood and motioned toward the trees.

"She's telling the truth. There were two people here, one slight, one heavier, larger. The bigger one—"

"The cop," Damien spit, as if it was an obscenity.

"He lost a lot of blood." He trained the light on the grass again, back to the boulder. "He must have climbed up here, used some kind of stick to push himself to his feet." The light bounced and moved across the rocks, the grass, then toward the stand of trees where she'd gone. "She went that way. He followed."

She sucked in a breath. He'd found Adam's trail? Adam had followed her?

"Back in the buggy," Damien ordered.

Ned hopped over the side and the buggy took off, straight for the trees where she'd run. And, apparently, unbeknownst to her until now, where Adam had gone, too. That must be where he was hiding. And she'd led them straight to him.

She pressed a hand to her throat. What had she done?

Chapter Twelve

Like a rubbernecker on the highway, unable to look away from the scene of an accident in spite of being horrified, Jody stared at the beam of Ned's flashlight as it got smaller and smaller in the distance. Her relief that Adam had not been hiding behind any of the trees in this part of the bald had been short-lived. Like a bloodhound, Ned had easily picked up his trail again, leading straight toward the water.

While she sat in the front passenger seat of the buggy, her hands going numb tied to the roll bar above her, Owen continued to whine in the back seat.

"Why can't I help search for him? I'm just as good a tracker as he is."

"Oh, really?" Damien clutched the steering wheel with his good hand and stared at Owen in the mirror. "When's the last time you tracked anything, or anyone?"

"I tracked that Tracy girl down just fine. It may have been in town instead of mountains. But I tracked her good."

Jody stiffened and looked at Damien. He was staring

at her now, probably waiting for her reaction. A slow, cruel smile curved his lips.

"That you did, little brother. Guess I forgot about that. Still, it wasn't like she got very far before we'd realized she took off. And it wasn't at night, so it was a lot easier to recapture her."

Recapture? Had Tracy escaped, only to be caught again? "Where is she?" Jody demanded. "What have you done to her?"

"You really want to know?"

She nodded.

"Then tell me where your boss keeps the rest of his surveillance equipment. Where are the other pictures and videos? Audio recordings?"

"I told you, I don't know of anywhere else he would keep anything. As far as I know, he always keeps it at the office. I don't even think he took his work home with him. It…it was a habit from when his wife was still alive. She made him promise to leave work at the office, literally and figuratively. So both of them could relax and not think about their cases when the work-day was over."

"Ah, now. Isn't that sweet?" He leaned toward her, forcing her to press herself against the door to the limits of her bound hands above her. "Tell you a secret, honey. He didn't keep his promise to that dear old lady of his. We found plenty of work files and pictures at his house." His smile faded. "Just not the right ones."

"You…you went to his house?"

He grinned again and relaxed against the seat. "Don't

worry. It's not like Sammy boy cares anymore." His laughter made her stomach clench with dread.

Please be bluffing. Please don't have hurt Sam.

Owen chuckled in the back seat, as if the two of them shared a private joke.

"Where's Sam?" she asked, her throat tight. "Please tell me you didn't hurt him."

"Well, now. I would, but then, I wouldn't want to lie."

Bile rose in her throat as Owen and Damien both laughed. Damien hadn't mentioned using Sam as leverage, only Tracy. And from what he'd just said, he wasn't even trying to pretend that Sam was okay. Or was he just saying that, making her think Sam was…that he *wasn't* okay, to make her scared of what he might do to her if she didn't talk? She had to cling to the hope that the dear old man who'd been like a father to her was still alive. She wouldn't be able to function otherwise.

She swallowed and drew a steadying breath. Tracy was still alive. Wasn't she? He was still using her friend as a bargaining chip. She *had* to be alive.

She stared through the windshield toward the water, moonlight sparkling off the little eddies and ripples caused by boulders just beneath the surface as the current rushed over them. Adam was out there somewhere, hopefully okay and hiding. Had he seen Ned? Did he know about both dune buggies loaded with thugs with guns? There was no way he could fight off all of Damien's men with only one pistol.

Don't worry about me, Adam. There's nothing you can do to save me. Don't be a hero. Don't get yourself killed.

The portable two-way radio sitting in the console crackled, startling her.

"It's Ned. Pick up."

Damien grabbed the radio and clicked the button on the side. "Damien here. Go ahead."

"His trail leads directly to the water and stops. Either he fell in or he went in on purpose." Ned's voice, deadly calm and matter-of-fact, sounded through the speaker.

Damien swore. "I want that cop. If he drowned, I want his body as proof. He's seen my face, my jailhouse ink. He knows I'm an ex-con. If he makes it back to civilization, he'll eventually figure out who I am. Once he does, if he pulls the wrong thread, connects the right dots, you can kiss your cut bye-bye. You got me?"

"Understood."

They were talking about killing Adam as if they were making a grocery list. Who *were* these people?

"What's your theory?" Damien asked through the radio.

"If he didn't fall in, he could be walking in the shallow part to keep from leaving a blood trail. With a wound like his, and judging by the blood he lost back at that boulder, I don't see him doing much more than that. The stream is too wide, the current too fast, for an injured man to cross to the other side. But I don't know this guy, how strong or motivated he might be. We'll need to check the far side, just to be sure."

"Owen can do that."

"Bro, I don't want to swim across a freezing-cold stream. Make someone else—"

"Shut up, Owen. Get out of the buggy."

Owen cursed a blue streak, but he popped the door open and got out. His boots crunched on some rocks just outside the car as he started down the rise toward the water.

"What else do you need?" Damien asked through the mic.

"If I'm going hunting, I'll need my pack, plenty of ammo for my nine millimeter and the rifle."

"Owen." Damien motioned to the other man, who stopped to look at him. "Get back here."

When Owen trudged to the driver's side, Damien gestured with his thumb to the back seat. "Get Ned's backpack for him. And your rifle and ammo. Get some nine-millimeter magazines, too."

"My rifle? He's got a pistol. Why's he want my rifle?"

Damien narrowed his eyes. "Who bought that rifle for you? Like I buy everything else?"

Owen threw his hands up in the air. "Fine. Whatever. I'll get it."

When Owen was jogging down the hillside again, this time with a backpack and rifle, Damien turned in his seat to face Jody. "Don't worry. They'll find him."

He chuckled, as if amused by her distress. But any sign of humor quickly faded as he stared at her. "You've wasted my time all day and caused me way more trouble than you're worth." He motioned toward the sling that immobilized his left arm. "I haven't forgotten that I owe you for this. But I'm willing to forgive this one time, if you give me what I want. Normally I'm a patient guy." He chuckled again, which clearly meant he *wasn't.* "But that little PI firm of yours has been a thorn in my side for three days. And I didn't have time to spare to begin with. Where are the rest of the pictures? You want that friend of yours to live, then tell me what I need to know."

She raised her chin, trying to act brave even though inside she wanted to curl up into a fetal position. "Which friend? Sam, Tracy or Adam?" She swallowed, every muscle tensed as she waited for his answer.

His brows arched up. "Well, now. That's a question, isn't it? I think we both know that Sam's a lost cause at this point." He winked and grinned when she pressed her lips together to keep from crying out.

Sam. Oh no, Sam.

"I admit, I might have been a little hasty with your boss." He let out a laborious sigh. "Regrets can be a terrible thing. Interrogating him first would have saved me a lot of trouble, for sure. As for that cop of yours, well, once again, lost cause. He's not getting out of here alive. That's not negotiable. I've got big plans, and him mouthing off to other law enforcement pigs could ruin everything. I'm not letting that happen. Guess that leaves you with just one friend to be worried about. Your fellow office worker, that Amazon warrior woman with legs that go all the way up. Tall women aren't normally my taste. But she's got some curves, nice melons. I could enjoy some of that. What's her name? Tracy? Yeah, that's it. Tracy Larson. You worried about her?" He leaned forward, his eyes blazing with menace. "Because you should be."

Her stomach clenched, and she pressed back against the door. "Where is she?"

"In safekeeping, for now. But only if you start talking. My infamous patience is about gone. Where are the recordings?"

She flexed her bound hands, which were tingling in the night chill with them tied above her head. "They have to be in Sam's office. That's where he keeps everything."

"Yeah, well, not this time. I've tossed that place high and low, went through every SD card and flash drive I could find. You and that Tracy girl are the only two other people who worked there. So it's up to you to spill the beans."

"What...what makes you so sure there are more recordings?"

He rolled his eyes. "You think I'm dumb? Your boss had date and time stamps on all of his pictures. And there's a gap in them, on a very specific day. He was watching us for a whole week based on the other time stamps. And there's one day smack-dab in the middle that's missing. Tell me where the rest of the stuff is and I'm gone, like I was never here. You'll never see me again. Promise."

She could feel the blood draining from her face. He might have thought his little speech would convince her that Tracy was still alive, that if she gave him what he wanted, she could still save her friend. But after hearing his callous talk about Sam and Adam, and fitting the pieces together, she realized she'd been kidding herself all this time.

Damien's tactics were to kill first, ask questions later. After killing Sam, he'd realized he'd made a mistake. So he'd taken Tracy. He'd no doubt *interrogated* her, and when Tracy had nothing to share, he'd likely killed her. That was the only reason Jody could come up with for why *she* was still sitting here, alive, relatively unhurt. She was Damien's last chance to get the information he needed. He had to make sure it was secured, maybe destroyed, so no one else would find it. And once he did that, he'd kill her to keep her from talking.

"Good," he said. "You're obviously thinking hard about what I've said. Just hurry it up. Your friend's life, and yours, depends on it. If you take too long, I'll order her killed and cut the truth out of your flesh. You feel me, girl?" He didn't wait for her reply. He turned away and stared toward the water.

Tears burned the backs of Jody's eyes as she followed his gaze. She hated that she cried so easily. But in this case, maybe it had helped her. Damien had to have seen the tears she was trying so hard to hold back and figured she was on the verge of breaking and telling him what he needed to know.

He was right, of course.

She wasn't a strong person, never had been. If she had any clue where other recordings or pictures were, she'd probably have spewed that information back on the Sugarland Mountain Trail. And he would have killed her right then.

She blinked hard, forcing the tears back. If she'd died up on that trail, Adam would have found a dead body instead of ever seeing Damien. He'd be sitting in an office somewhere investigating her death, or maybe others would take on that chore while he went off to do whatever it was law enforcement rangers did. The important thing was that he'd be safe, having never become a target of Damien's wrath.

She clenched her fingers together, trying to keep the blood flowing as she looked through the windshield in the same direction where Damien was looking—down at the water. The second dune buggy was parked by the river now. Flashlight beams pointed down at the ground as the four men from that buggy, plus Ned and Owen, searched for Adam. Six men searching for one, all so they could ensure his silence, that he'd never tell anyone about Damien. Any doubts she'd had about Tracy maybe still being alive died a quick death.

The man beside her didn't value life. And he didn't like being inconvenienced. He'd shot and killed one of his own men to keep him from talking, or maybe to save himself the trouble of dragging him to safety. He was being greatly inconvenienced by Jody right now. No way would he do that if he had another option.

Her best friend in the whole world was dead. And Adam McKenzie—an honorable, kind man willing to risk everything to save a stranger—was going to be dead, too, if she didn't do something to help him. Assuming he wasn't dead already, lying on the bald somewhere, his wound torn open and bleeding out. But what could she do? How could she help him?

She wasn't lying about the pictures. She really didn't know where Sam might have hidden them if he'd stumbled onto something bad and wanted to hide it from her and Tracy for some reason. So where did that leave her?

For the moment, it left her with leverage. As long as this bloodthirsty idiot beside her thought she could give him what he wanted, he'd keep her alive. She could make something up, bluff, buy some time. He'd kill her anyway. Not much she could do about that. But if she could buy Adam some time, maybe, just maybe, with his law enforcement experience and knowledge of these mountains, maybe that would be enough to let him get away and get some help…and survive.

If the legacy of her twenty-four short years on this planet was that she managed to save Adam McKenzie's life, well, that wouldn't be too bad. She could take comfort in that—if she could make it happen.

She watched the lights in the distance. They were still searching, which meant they hadn't caught Adam yet. If he'd passed out from blood loss, they would have found his body by now, wouldn't they? So he was still alive. There was still time to save him.

While she watched the flashlights bobbing through the trees that lined the stream, she came up with a plan. Not a very good one, but better than nothing.

"Damien?"

He frowned and looked at her, obviously not pleased with her using his name. "What?"

"I'll… I'm willing to show you where the other pictures are. But I have conditions."

He grabbed her chin and squeezed it in a painful grip. "How about this condition? You tell me what I need to know. Period. And then maybe I don't kill you."

She jerked her head, but he only tightened his fingers, the nails biting into her skin.

"Kill me and those pictures will be found and made public. I guarantee it. I'm the one in charge of storing all our case files. And part of that responsibility is making sure the files are sent back to Sam if something happens to me. It's…it's in my will, the location of those files. It'll all come out. Whoever handles Sam's estate will get the files. Then they'll be made public."

"You're lying. You're a kid, probably fresh out of college. You don't even have a will."

"Oh, really? I'm a criminal justice major and I work for a private investigator. You think my professors, and Sam, didn't drill into me the importance of ensuring that I have a will, and that any important documents are preserved and turned over to the executor of that will upon my death?"

She wasn't lying about that. Her professors and Sam *had* drilled that information into her. But the glaring flaw in her story was that the papers, and pictures, that she'd mentioned in her will were of course her own, not Sam's. Her storage unit was full of her cameras and SD cards and file cabinets loaded with pictures that she'd taken as part of her other job, as a professional photographer. She had mentioned the unit in her will and left a copy of her key with the lawyer who'd drawn it up. That was part of securing *her* assets. Not Sam's.

But Damien didn't know that.

If she could get him to believe her now, and take her to her storage unit, he could spend days going through all her SD cards looking for the specific pictures he believed to be there. That would buy her a little time, hopefully enough to escape. If not, maybe she'd at least be able to get a note under a door to another storage unit, or somehow leave it for someone else to find, a note that would let them know about Adam so they could send him help.

"Load up your guys into the buggies and take me back to town. If you do that, if you leave Adam alone, I'll take you to where the pictures are stored. And you'll let Tracy go. She's safe and sound, like you said, right?"

She bit her bottom lip, trying to look hopeful, even though she was convinced that her friend was already dead.

He straightened in his seat. "Sure, sure. She's safe and sound. I'll take you back to town, get the pictures and both of you will go free."

"And Ranger McKenzie? What about him?"

His jaw tightened. "He's a threat to me, him being a cop and all." His gaze darted back and forth as he appeared to consider her deal. "Okay, my plans will be taken care of in the next few days. I can pull my guys back, have them watch the trails to make sure your cop doesn't find his way back, for two days. After that, it won't matter. We'll be gone. Of course, I'll have to accommodate you as a guest for those two days as well. You understand. But after that, I'll let you go—if you take me to the pictures."

"And Tracy? You'll let her go, too?"

"Oh, right, right. Her too. Do we have a deal?"

Her heart shattered at how casual he was about Tracy. He'd already forgotten about her. It was so hard to keep up her pretense without giving in to grief, to pretend she was buying the snake oil this viper was selling. "Cut my hands free and we'll shake on it."

He snickered. "No can do. You'll try to get away."

"It's not like we can drive back into Gatlinburg with my hands tied to the roll bar. I'm not going to try to escape. I'm not betting Adam's or Tracy's lives on that."

"I'll cross that bridge when we get there. Your hands stay tied."

She shrugged, as if it didn't matter. Her hands really were going numb. But mainly she'd wanted them free to give her more options. Like maybe she could grab his gun. But he was too careful for that.

"We have a deal?" she asked.

"We do."

She nodded toward the stream. "Your men?"

"Oh, of course." He was all smiles and acting like her friend now that he thought he was going to get what he wanted.

He radioed the change in plans. "Got that, boys?"

"Got it, boss," Owen answered.

Damien frowned. "Why do you have the radio instead of Ned?"

A pause, then, "Ned was worried the chatter would warn the cop. He didn't want the radio. He gave it to me so he could track him."

As Damien took the opportunity to tell Owen what an idiot he thought he was, Jody tried to focus on the coming challenge, how to draw the time out once they got to the storage unit. Was there something she could use inside to try to get word to someone to come help

Adam? Not that she believed that Damien would truly follow through, that he'd pull all of his men off the search permanently. He'd said "your cut" earlier, which implied there was money riding on whatever Sam had seen. He wasn't going to risk Adam making it out of here and ruining that. But at least getting them all out of these mountains for the time being, until Damien could get more men out here searching, would give Adam a head start.

The lawn mower–type roar of the second buggy started up in the distance. All she could see were the beams from flashlights bouncing around as, she assumed, the men got into the buggy. Then the flashlights flicked off. She could tell there were men in the buggy. But she had no way of counting them from this far away.

"Looks like they're ready," Damien announced. "They'll follow us out of the mountains, like I promised." He started up the engine. It sputtered then caught, adding its dull, throaty roar to the sound of the other buggy that was idling down by the water and hadn't yet moved.

"I need to see them," she insisted. "I need to see six men in that buggy. Then *they* can take the lead. We'll follow them out. I have to make sure they're all there, that none of them are looking for Adam."

His eyes narrowed. "You thinking I ain't holding up my end of our deal? You calling me a liar?"

"Trust but verify."

He surprised her by laughing. "You're a lot more like me than you probably think you are. Wheeling and dealing, probably lying but playing the innocent."

He laughed again. "You think I don't see that hamster wheel spinning around in your head a hundred miles an hour? You think you're clever, getting me to call off the search and let you and your friend go. If I thought there was a good chance of your boyfriend making it out of here in the next twenty-four hours, I wouldn't go along with whatever game you're playing. Just make sure you haven't outsmarted yourself. 'Cause if you don't take me to those pictures, I'm not drawing this out any longer. I'll slit your throat and take my chances. And I'll come back here personally and kill that cop."

He floored the gas and the buggy took off, bumping over the rocky field.

Jody squinted toward the other buggy, trying to make out the different silhouettes. The one in the driver's seat was most likely Owen, because he was leaning back against the headrest as if bored, probably whining to everyone else about being cold or something. The others seemed to have their backs to them, looking out at the water.

She tensed. Had they seen something? If Adam was hiding and had made some kind of noise, would they draw their weapons and shoot him, in spite of the fragile deal she had with Damien?

The buggy pulled to a stop perpendicular to the other one, headlights illuminating the group of men.

Jody sucked in a shocked breath.

"What the—" Damien stood up in his seat to get a better view.

There weren't six men in the buggy. There were only five. Ned was missing. But the rest of them were bound and gagged, including Owen. Their own clothes had been used to tie them up. All of them were shirtless. Shoestrings tied their hands together.

Damien let out a guttural roar of rage and slammed the gas, whipping the steering wheel hard left. The buggy spun in the dirt, then took off in the direction of the Sugarland Trail, leaving a wide-eyed and gagged Owen behind along with the other men. A tree loomed up ahead. Damien turned the wheel to avoid it. The headlights suddenly revealed a man standing in their path, about fifty yards ahead, aiming a rifle directly at them.

It was Adam. He was alive!

Damien floored the gas, heading right for him.

Chapter Thirteen

The dune buggy barreled down on Adam. He didn't move out of the way. He carefully aimed his rifle at the driver's side of the windshield, painfully aware that Jody was just a few feet away from the driver. He squeezed the trigger.

Bam!

He heard the crack of the windshield and guttural cursing from behind the blinding headlights. Had he hit Damien? Had he hit Jody? That possibility had his stomach clenching with dread. But he'd had to take the shot. If he let Damien take her out of these mountains, she was as good as dead. He'd had to risk it.

The buggy was still barreling down on him. He aimed for the driver's side headlight, then lowered the rifle bore to just beneath it, going for the tire.

Bam! Whoosh!

The left front tire blew. The buggy hop-skipped sideways. The headlights arced away from him, and he got his first clear look at Jody. Her eyes were wide with fright, but she seemed okay. Relief flooded through him, but not for long. The buggy bounced like crazy, sliding toward him. Damien was wrestling for control with his one good arm, even as he shrugged off the sling on his bad arm. Moonlight glinted off the pistol clutched awkwardly in his left hand, pointing at Adam.

Adam leveled the rifle again.

"No!" Jody yelled. She yanked herself up in the air toward the roll bar and slammed her legs into Damien's shoulders. The pistol went flying.

Adam jerked his rifle up so he wouldn't hit her.

The buggy made a sickening lurch, then careened toward him.

Adam dived out of the way, rolling across the ground, the buggy coming to a bouncing stop about ten yards away, miraculously still upright.

His left leg was on fire, but he fought through the pain, limping as fast as he could to reach the buggy. He rounded the driver's seat, aiming his rifle inside. The seat was empty. Damien was gone.

"Where is he, Jody?"

She motioned with her chin. "He jumped out, ran toward the water."

Adam yanked his knife out of his boot and leaned across the opening. He sliced the rope on the roll bar, freeing her. "Can you drive?"

"The tire—"

"Don't make any sudden turns or stops and we should be able to ride on the rim for a bit on this soft ground. We have to get out of here, now, before Damien finds the cache of guns I took away from his men, or the one who took off looking for me returns. He would have heard the gunshots and could be back any second."

She was shaking her hands, working her fingers. "I'll

try. My hands feel like a thousand needles are stabbing them." She stepped over the middle console and plopped down behind the wheel. "What about you? How will you get into the—"

He rolled over the side of the buggy and fell into the back seat. "Go! Head that way." He motioned toward where they'd come from earlier in the day, back toward the Sugarland Trail.

"Your leg. Are you okay? How did you—"

Boom!

The crack of another rifle sounded from the direction of the water.

"Go, go, go!" Adam yelled even as he returned fire.

The buggy took off, tilting dangerously to the right.

"Back off the gas, ease into it!" Adam fired several more rounds, laying cover fire as Jody brought the buggy under control, then took off more slowly.

The buggy straightened out, the ride so bumpy and lopsided that Adam fell back. He scrambled across the seat on his knees, cursing when his makeshift splint caught on a seat belt and pulled his hurt leg. Fire shot up to his thigh, but he couldn't give in to the pain now. He gritted his teeth and brought up his rifle, exchanging shot after shot with the thugs by the other buggy until it fell out of sight behind a rise.

He collapsed, clutching his useless leg.

Jody looked at him in the mirror. "Should I pull over?"

"No! Keep going. I slashed all four tires in the other vehicle and tossed the keys in the water. That should give us a good chance. But it's still a dune buggy. They can ride it with flat tires on this ground just like we're doing. All it takes is one guy who knows how to hot-wire it and they'll be after us in no time."

"Then…what can we do? This buggy can't get back up the mountain where we came down. I don't remember a road."

"There's a road—several. Access roads we rangers use, more like wide footpaths than roads, but they'll do the job. I assume Damien and his men came down one of them to get to us as fast they did. We'll have to keep ahead of them. That's our best chance right now."

A dull roar sounded in the distance. The other buggy, back over the rise they'd just come down.

Jody's tortured gaze met his again in the mirror. "Is there a plan B?"

This was his plan B. Plan A had pretty much ended when he'd had to shoot out the buggy tire to get Damien to stop. He'd hoped to use that buggy for his and Jody's escape. Without a flat tire, they could be going twice as fast as they were now, and escape would have been easy.

He forced a smile even though his leg was throbbing so hard he could barely think straight. And it was bleeding again. And he was pretty sure he was close to passing out. Again. "I'll think of something."

A bright spotlight popped on ahead of them.

Jody slammed the brakes.

Adam grabbed the roll bar and swung himself into the seat beside her, dropping onto his knees and aiming his rifle straight ahead over the top of the windshield.

They came to a shuddering stop, turned sideways, with Adam's side the one facing the lights.

"Drop your weapon!" a voice called out over a loud-speaker.

Adam hesitated.

The spotlight swept off to the side, still lighting up the buggy but not in his eyes anymore. He got his first clear glimpse at what they were facing. A group of at least fifteen men and women formed a semicircle about a hundred feet away. They were all aiming rifles at them.

"Drop it!" the voice ordered again.

Adam pitched his rifle out and held his hands up in the air.

Jody stared at him in shock. "What are you doing?"

He was about to tell her when the loudspeaker buzzed again. "Step out of the vehicle, hands up."

"Go ahead," he told her. "These are—"

Chh-chh. Four men materialized from out of the darkness on either side of them. One had just pumped his shotgun.

"Put the guns away," Adam told them, sounding furious as he leaned over Jody as if to shield her. "I'm Ranger Adam McKenzie."

"Lower your weapons!" Another man jogged into view, shaking his head as he reached the buggy. "What have you gotten yourself into this time, Adam?"

Jody's eyes were wide, her face pale as she looked back and forth between them, her hands in the air.

Adam rolled his eyes at him, but he couldn't help but grin as he gently pressed Jody's arms down. "Jody Ingram, meet National Park Service Investigative Officer, Special Agent Duncan McKenzie. My brother."

Chapter Fourteen

Adam looked over his brother's head, past the foot of the hospital bed to where Jody was curled into a completely uncomfortable-looking chair by the window, passed out from exhaustion.

"Earth to Adam," Duncan said. "She's fine. The doctor checked her out last night, and other than some bumps and bruises, she's okay. You can quit checking on her every thirty seconds."

Adam shoved his brother's arm off the bed railing. "And you can stop exaggerating. I've only checked on her a few times since you came in."

"Yeah. Whatever." He didn't look convinced as he waved a hand toward Adam's left leg, heavily bandaged and propped up on some pillows. "I'm surprised they didn't cut that thing off while I was dealing with your mountain buddies all morning." He winced with sympathy. "It looked awful yesterday. Had to hurt like a son of a gun. What's the prognosis?"

He started to glance at Jody again but caught himself.

Duncan grinned, as if he could read his mind. Maybe he could. The two of them were the closest in age of all of his brothers. They were only ten months apart—Irish twins, as the saying went. Most strangers had difficulty telling them apart. Every time he had to tell someone in front of his mom that, no, they weren't twins, they were ten months apart, she'd blush bright red. His dad would grin with pride, as if his virility had been confirmed. He didn't mind at all being the stereotype behind the slang Irish twins saying that some found offensive. He just pointed to his other two sons and smiled. Or, most of the time to his other *one* son, since the fourth son was rarely ever home, doing everything he could to keep his title as the reigning black sheep of the family.

"The doctor threw all kinds of medical jargon at me. The best I can tell, I pretty much ripped the main muscles apart when I pulled that piece of wood out. Creating a makeshift splint out of tree branches and my shirt and chasing down the bad guys destroyed the rest. If I'm lucky and the antibiotics work like they're supposed to, I might get full use of the leg with a year or so of physical therapy."

Duncan winced again. "And if you're not lucky?"

Adam's hands tightened on the blanket covering him. "They lop it off." He shrugged. "Jody's alive. I'm alive. That's a miracle considering what we were up against. If I end up losing a leg out of it, I consider myself lucky."

"You have a warped view of good luck," Jody's soft, feminine voice called out from her window seat. "And there was no luck involved. You almost killed yourself saving both of us. If the National Park Service hands out medals, you deserve a drawer full of them."

She uncurled her legs and headed toward the bed.

She held her hand across Adam to the other side, offering it to his brother. "Thank you for rescuing us, Duncan. But knowing your brother, he'd have found a way to finish the job and bring us both home, even without your help. He's pretty amazing."

Duncan shook her hand. "I'm sure you're right, Miss Ingram. Adam would have found a way. He's a pretty resourceful guy and I'm proud to have him as a fellow officer, and a brother."

Adam rolled his eyes.

Duncan dropped down into his chair as Jody took the one on the other side of the bed. He picked up an electronic tablet from the bedside table and tapped the screen, bringing it to life. "I'm actually on duty, in spite of the obscenely late hour of seven on a Sunday evening—well past my normal dinnertime. I need to take Adam's statement now that he's finally out of surgery and no longer under the influence of anesthesia. My team's heading up the investigation in conjunction with the local police."

"So sorry to have inconvenienced you by having a long surgery," Adam said, rolling his eyes.

Duncan grinned.

"Have they found Tracy? Or Sam?" Jody asked.

"Not yet, ma'am. But I promise you we have every available resource searching for them. We've also got a team looking for that Damien fellow and his right-hand guy, Ned. The rest of them we captured and put into lockup, waiting to be processed. We know their names because of their fingerprints. They're all in the system. We just have to figure out last names for Damien and

Ned and make the connections, figure out how and why they ended up together. We're on this. Don't you worry."

She nodded her thanks and rubbed her hands up and down her arms, as if chilled.

Adam started to pull his blanket off to give to her.

She put her hand on his, stopping him. "Don't you dare. I'll go ask the nurse for an extra one. Be right back."

As soon as the door to the hospital room closed, Adam rolled his head on his pillow to look at his brother. "Waiting to be processed? No one has interrogated the thugs you captured?"

"Every single one lawyered up. We didn't get squat from any of them."

"Any idea what their connection is to each other?"

"Career criminals, and not the garden-variety street thugs, either. They all have long records with everything from grand theft auto to breaking and entering. One of them was charged with murder but beat the rap. No question he did it—the prosecutor made some stupid mistakes and he got off on a technicality. But finding links between them has proven difficult. If anything, the lack of links is what's so glaring and concerning. They've all done some time, either in jail or prison, but never at the same places, not at the same time, at least. Two of them aren't even from Tennessee. And the states they're from aren't the same, either. So, again, no links, other than them being lowlifes who will do anything for a buck."

Adam drew the obvious conclusions. "Damien's the leader, so he probably hired all the guys working for him. Instead of bringing on guys he did time with or knew in some way, he purposely went out of his way to hire strangers. He didn't want to risk anything coming back to point to him."

Duncan nodded. "That's my take, too. Which makes me think that either Damien has some kind of connection to whatever is behind the abductions, or someone who hired him does. And that someone is going to great lengths to distance themselves from whatever happens. Even if everything hits the fan, they want to come out lily-white."

"You think someone hired Damien? That he's not the one behind this?" Adam asked.

"Did he strike you as smart enough to mastermind all of this?"

"Hard to say. Didn't you find his fingerprints on the buggy he drove? He has to be in the system. Those were prison tattoos on his arms."

Duncan's mouth flattened. "Unfortunately, the steering wheel and the rest of the interior of the buggies isn't conducive to giving us viable sets of prints. They're textured, don't provide anything useful in the fingerprint department."

"What about the outside of the buggies, the painted surfaces? Can't you get prints off those?"

"Oh, we've got plenty of prints from the outside. So far, every one matches up to the guys we've already got locked up. Not one of them leads to this Damien guy. Also, the buggies were stolen. So tracing registration is a dead end."

"Figures." Adam blew out a breath in frustration.

"The lack of prints doesn't make sense. He wasn't wearing gloves. And I didn't see him wipe down anything. He sure didn't have time to later, when he took off running."

"If he took precautions to only touch the textured plastic door handle on the outside, he wouldn't have left prints. A guy who went to the care he did in order to hire guys who weren't connected to him in any way could have been careful enough to think about fingerprints before touching anything."

Adam stretched his leg, wincing when a sharp pain radiated up his calf. "You have to have a theory about all of this. A group of thugs kidnaps all three employees of a PI firm and threatens one of them if she doesn't show them where some supposed pictures are. Makes sense it's all related to one of Campbell's cases, don't you think?"

Duncan nodded. "The possibility has crossed my mind. This Damien fellow was worried about surveillance photos. The client who hired Sam would have wanted the photos taken. And there wouldn't be any reason for Sam to hide the photos from the guy paying his bills."

"So whoever was in the photos found out that the client hired a private investigator and wants any pictures he took. The question is how did the person in the photos find out. You think Sam got sloppy? That someone saw him taking pictures?"

"Seems like the simplest scenario, and it matches what Miss Ingram said on the chopper on the way to the hospital. Whoever is being followed by Sam sees him and hires Damien to kill Sam and hire a group of guys to toss Campbell's home and office. Only they're still searching the office when Tracy Larson goes to work, and she catches them in the act."

Adam nodded, following the scenario. "There's a struggle, maybe they kill her—either accidentally or on purpose—and then they realize the pictures they're looking for are nowhere to be found. Now they're getting desperate. Was there anything in Campbell's office to let them know that Jody worked there, too? And that she was the only remaining employee?"

"Absolutely. Campbell was meticulous. His payroll records were right in his filing cabinet. Damien knew there were three of them. Without Sam or Tracy around to interrogate, Miss Ingram was the last link to making sure those pictures never find their way into anyone's hands. That's why they went after her." He shrugged. "Makes sense as a hypothetical. But I have to keep an open mind and follow the evidence. We may be on a completely wrong track. If Miss Ingram can remember more details about what Damien and the others may have said in front of her when you weren't with her, that could give us the clues we need to make all the puzzle pieces fit," Duncan said.

"I assume you're talking to all of Campbell's clients?"

"Of course. We sent the files from the office to our team of investigators. They're following up with everyone who hired him in the past month. If we don't get any leads out of that, we'll go back further. Don't worry. We'll figure it out."

"What about finding Sam Campbell and Tracy Larson?" When his brother hesitated, Adam narrowed his eyes. "You found them, didn't you? That's what you really came in here to tell me. But since Jody was here you couldn't."

"I came in here to check on my brother and take a more detailed statement now that you're coherent and off drugs. But, yes, you're right. We found something. Or, rather, some*one*. A body. The autopsy isn't finished yet. They'll need DNA results or dental records to confirm the identity."

"Male or female?"

"Male."

"Sam Campbell."

Duncan nodded. "Most likely but it hasn't been confirmed. Physical description and approximate age matches the body, and there aren't any other open missing-persons cases that could fit. He was dumped in a ditch not far from his office, beside a rural road. Critters and decomp took their toll. Thus the need to wait for dental records or DNA results before making it official."

"Understood. What about her friend Tracy Larson?"

"Based on the quick statement you gave me while the search-and-rescue team hauled you two out in the chopper, I can't imagine that she's still alive. But without a body, we're still treating it as a search and rescue, not a recovery. Not yet."

"No leads?"

"None. Her car was parked at the office, so it seems likely that's where she was taken. No witnesses so far, though. We've canvassed her apartment complex, too, in case this was planned in advance and someone suspicious was hanging out watching her place in the week before she disappeared. Gatlinburg PD is doing a knock and talk, going door to door to follow up with anyone who wasn't home when they did their initial canvass. But the last reported sighting of Miss Larson so far is Friday afternoon, when Miss Ingram left the office."

"I prefer Jody to Miss Ingram."

They both looked toward the door. Jody was just inside, her face pale, her freckles standing out in stark relief.

"How long have you been listening?" Adam asked.

Two bright spots of color darkened her cheeks as she clutched a beige blanket in her arms. "I wasn't purposely trying to eavesdrop. I was about to step inside when I heard you mention Tracy. I didn't want to interrupt, or make you stop, because everyone has been so tight-lipped. It's frustrating. No one seems to want to tell me anything."

She stepped to the plastic chair on Adam's right and sat down, bringing the blanket up to her chin.

Adam exchanged a relieved looked with his brother. If Jody had only started listening at the mention of Tracy, then she hadn't heard that a body had been found and might be Sam. He wanted to keep it that way until the coroner confirmed the identity. "Duncan, can you—"

"Yeah, yeah." He set the tablet on the table and stood. "I'll give you both a few minutes. But then I really need that statement."

"Make it ten."

Duncan nodded. "Ten it is. I'll bring back some coffee. Miss Ingram—"

"Jody."

He smiled broadly, pouring on the charm. "Jody. Lovely name for a fine, Irish-looking lass. Your red hair and green eyes are a perfect foil to black Irish here, with those blue eyes and black hair."

"You have the same blue eyes and black hair," Adam growled. "And stop with the fake accent. You've never even been to Ireland."

Duncan's grin widened as he continued to stare at Jody. "How do you take your coffee, sweet colleen?"

Adam wanted to strangle him.

Jody smiled. "Cream and sugar, please."

"My pleasure." He headed out of the room.

"Is he always that cheeky?" she asked.

Adam blinked. "Cheeky? Are you going to start talking in a British accent now?"

"I bloody well might," she teased, her inflections a perfect imitation of an English lady's, even if the language she used wasn't.

"Don't fall for his *cheekiness*," he said. "He's married to his job."

"And you aren't?"

He shook his head. "Haven't been on the job long enough to be married to it yet. I transferred from Memphis a few months ago." He held his right hand out, unable to resist the need to touch her, to remind himself there was still some good left in this world. There were many dark times, like now, when he wasn't so sure.

There was no hesitation on her part. She slid her hand through the large opening in the railing. She entwined her fingers with his and rested their joined hands on the mattress.

He squeezed reassuringly and searched her face. She was dressed in clothes a policewoman had brought from her apartment, another white blouse—that unfortunately had all its buttons—and a pair of faded jeans that hugged the curves of her hips and offered a tempting view of her backside whenever she walked across the room. He had availed himself of that view far too often since waking up from recovery to find her in his room this afternoon.

He cleared his throat, forcing himself to focus on the case, not his ridiculous fascination with the beautiful woman just a few feet away. "I'm sorry you heard that, about Tracy. No one has given up hope. They're still searching for her."

She nodded, looking sad but resigned. "You don't think she's alive any more than I do. Even from the beginning, as soon as you heard about her and knew that Damien had confronted me on the trail. You put the pieces together pretty fast, figured out that Damien would have killed me to eliminate witnesses if Tracy was still alive and could tell him what he needed."

He wanted to lie. But she deserved better than that, and she was too smart to fall for it anyway. "You're right. I figured he was eliminating witnesses to whatever he was trying to hide right from the get-go. He didn't strike me as the ruminating type. Act first, regret later. That seems to be his motto." He squeezed her fingers again. "But miracles do happen. Maybe instead of…well, maybe Tracy escaped after all. Damien may have gone after you because you were his last lead and he was desperate to make sure the pictures don't fall into someone else's hands. Your friend may be hiding somewhere this very minute, not sure where to go or what to do. I guarantee she's got the very best possible men and women out trying to find her, both in the mountains and in town. No one's giving up."

She nodded her thanks and pulled her hand free to tug the blanket up higher around her where it had started to fall. The loss of her touch sent a sharp pang of longing through him. He had to force himself not to reach for her again. She was too good for him. There was no chance of a future between them, in spite of the attraction that seemed to simmer every time she was in the same room—a mutual attraction, judging by the hungry looks she'd been casting his way all afternoon as he'd endured exams and bandage changes and listened to long lectures from his doctor on what to do and what not to do.

He frowned and waved at her clothing. "Your hospital gown is gone. I'm assuming they discharged you after keeping you for observation last night. Where do you plan on going when you leave?"

"One of the police officers brought me a key to my apartment that she got from the manager. I guess I'll go there—home. And before you say it, I'm sure I'll be okay. My Glock is locked up there. If Damien or Ned or any other thugs he wants to send after me show up, they won't find a defenseless woman waiting for them.

And I've got a phone again if I needed to call for help. A victim's advocate that one of your people called gave me some cash and a pay-as-you-go cell phone from the hospital gift shop to replace mine."

"None of that sounds especially comforting. What about transportation?"

"I can call a cab. You don't have to worry about me. I'll be okay."

"You need protection. Have you asked the police—"

She laughed, without humor. "They're great and all. But they have a limited budget and can't afford to assign officers to watch over witnesses who may or may not be in danger. Especially when half the Park Service is out searching for the guys I'm allegedly in danger from. Apparently, the odds of them being able to get to me are extremely low."

"Is that a direct quote from some jerk police officer?"

"Pretty much. But to be fair, Gatlinburg PD and the Park Service have been great. It was only one jerk. And it's not anyone's fault that they have a limited budget. If I need protection, I've been told to hire my own."

He stared at his bum leg, hating himself for that one unguarded moment when he hadn't been careful enough and had stepped into a hole. "Will you? Hire someone?"

"I have a limited budget, too."

"When Duncan gets back, I'll tell him to withdraw some money from my account. I can hire someone to guard you for a few days."

She was already shaking her head before he finished. "No. Thank you very much, Adam. But you don't owe me anything. There's no reason for you to spend your money on me."

"I could make it a loan. With a really long payback time frame. Like forever."

She smiled. "You're amazing, you know that? But, like I said. I'll be fine. Now that I know to be careful, I'll be on my guard. And I'll keep my gun beside me tonight, ready to grab. Plus my phone. My apartment's just five minutes from the police station. Seriously, there's nothing to worry about. But thanks, just the same, for being concerned."

"I know you aren't close with your adoptive family. But surely they'd let you stay with them for a while. Wouldn't they?"

She stiffened, but before she could answer, the door clicked open and Duncan stepped inside. As soon as Adam saw the look on his brother's face, he reached for Jody's hand. She clutched it like a lifeline, her face pale as she waited for Duncan to speak.

"I'm so sorry, Jody. They found your friend Tracy Larson. She's dead."

Chapter Fifteen

Jody dried her face with a washcloth and stared at her reflection above the sink in Adam's hospital bathroom.

They found your friend Tracy Larson. She's dead.

Even though she'd been expecting those words, her heart didn't want to accept the truth.

She could see Tracy in her mind's eye, hear her voice, feel her arms around her whenever she'd needed a hug. Which was a whole lot more often than her strong, beautiful friend had ever needed. Tracy was a rock, always had been. Jody had been her weak, needy friend. During the most difficult years of Jody's life, Tracy and her family had been her comfort, her solace, her refuge from the storm. Jody would never have survived if it weren't for their love and support.

She swiped at her tears and straightened her shoulders. Hiding in this bathroom wasn't helping anyone. It was time to pull herself together and tell Adam and his brother everything she could remember about Damien and his thugs. Hopefully some of the details that were coming back to her now that she had finally gotten some sleep would provide the clues necessary to bring justice to her friend, and to Sam, if he too was dead, as Damien had taunted.

She opened the door and stepped out. Two very similar pairs of deep blue eyes looked at her with concern. She forced a smile and stepped around Duncan to take her seat beside Adam's bed.

"I want to help you catch Damien," she told Duncan. "I know that my earlier statement wasn't all that useful. I was exhausted and wasn't thinking straight. But I'm remembering more details now. Like that Damien and Owen are brothers."

Adam and Duncan exchanged a surprised look. "Brothers?" they echoed each other.

"I think so. In the buggy, Damien called Owen his little brother. He only said it once. It could have been a nickname. But if it wasn't, that could help you figure out more about Damien. Right?"

"Absolutely." Duncan pulled out his cell phone and started texting someone. A few moments later, he gave Jody a big smile. "Bingo. My guy brought up Owen Flint's bio. We knew he had a brother, Raymond D. Flint. But hadn't made the connection yet. The D stands for Damien." He held up his phone and turned it around. "Mugshot look familiar?"

"That's him," they both said.

"That's Damien," Jody confirmed. "He's the one who sent those men to kill Adam."

"And *you*," Adam said, frowning.

"Do you remember any other details you didn't mention before?" Duncan asked.

"Three days," she said. "It was part of that same conversation in the buggy. Damien said Sam's PI business had been causing him problems for three days. He had plans, big plans, and Owen wouldn't get his cut if Adam made it out of the mountains and connected the dots."

Adam and Duncan exchanged another look.

"Big plans?" Duncan asked.

"Connected the dots?" Adam asked.

She nodded. "They didn't talk about his plans or what he meant, other than that Adam was a cop and knew he was an ex-con—"

"Because of the tattoos," Adam said.

"I think so, yes. He was worried you'd figure out who he was before he could do whatever it is that he's planning."

"Are you looking at all of Sam Campbell's active cases?" Adam asked his brother.

"His office was crammed with hundreds of case files. We're using his planner to reconstruct a timeline for last week to start, so we can determine which cases he was actively working. So far we're up to twenty."

"He was meticulous with that planner," Jody said. "If he worked a case last week, it's definitely written down."

"Good to know. On the chopper when we were flying you and Adam to the hospital, you said that Damien insisted there were some pictures missing from Sam's office. Any idea why he thought any were missing? And where Sam might have put them?"

"I don't know where Sam would have put them other than the office. But as for thinking some were missing, I imagine Damien was referring to time stamps. I'm not sure if he meant actual dates and times printed on the photos, like I put on most of the pictures that I take for brochures before processing them through an editing program. He might have been referring to the metadata on SD cards that tell you when each picture was taken."

"Photography?" Adam asked. "Is that the second job you mentioned in the mountains? You work for a studio?"

"I work for myself, as far as the pictures are concerned. Sam couldn't afford to hire me full-time. So I run my own photography business on the side. Actually, calling it a business is probably stretching it. I get my clients through word of mouth. I don't have an office or anything like that."

"What do you do, exactly?" Adam asked.

"Work with hotels and cabin rental companies mainly, taking pictures and creating ads and brochures they can use to target tourists." She glanced back and forth between them. "If you're thinking some of Sam's photos could be mixed with mine, I assure you, the chances of that happening are zero."

"How can you be that positive?" Duncan asked.

"Because my photography work is run out of my apartment and a storage unit outside town. And Sam would never allow someone to bring work home. He likes to keep everything under lock and key at the office."

"Assuming you're right—"

"I am." She arched a brow at Duncan.

He smiled. "Okay. Then does Sam have a habit of

losing pictures at the office? Maybe putting them in the wrong files?"

She shook her head. "Not in the six months that I've been working there. He's extremely detail oriented, and careful. He'd keep all of the pictures for one case together. It doesn't make sense that any could have been misplaced."

Adam rubbed his left leg as if to try to ease the ache. "It makes sense if Sam purposely put the pictures somewhere else for safekeeping. Maybe he realized he had something important and was checking on some details before going to the police."

Duncan picked his computer tablet up from the table beside the bed. "Looks like it's going to be a long night for us investigators. We should have a preliminary timeline put together by morning. If you don't mind reviewing it, to make sure it looks right, I can bring it to you tomorrow. Does that work for you, Jody?"

"Of course. They've already discharged me from the hospital. I'll take a cab to my apartment in a little while. The address is—"

"No way are you going home," Adam interrupted. "It's not safe."

"I agree," Duncan said. "Damien and his men are likely looking for you. It's too dangerous. You should go to a hotel until we have him locked up."

She laughed. "Seriously? Did you miss the part where I work two jobs to make ends meet? I live paycheck to paycheck. If I have to pay for a hotel, I don't eat for a week."

"Not a problem," Adam said. "The doctor is discharging me later today. You can stay at my place."

Chapter Sixteen

Adam had expected Jody's apartment to be small. He hadn't expected it to be the size of one of those tiny houses that were all the rage on TV these days. Jody's apartment wasn't even a one-bedroom. It was an efficiency. She didn't have a bed. She had a day bed. If she'd had a couch, there wouldn't have been room for it. She had a lawn chair pulled up to a cardboard box, which apparently acted as her desk.

"Well," he said. "This is…cozy."

"I think you mean minuscule. Now you can see why I keep my cameras and equipment in a storage unit. My goal is to eventually get a full-time job as an investigator with the prosecutor's office. But until that miraculous day happens, I'm stuck in an efficiency."

She opened a door on the far wall, revealing a tiny closet. "I'll pack a bag and grab my Glock from the gun safe. Then we can take that fancy limo you rented and go to your place. Where do you live?"

He was about to answer when he realized she was pulling articles of clothing out of open boxes neatly lined up beneath her hanging clothes and shoving them into what amounted to a large book bag. She didn't even have a chest of drawers or a suitcase.

Thinking about his own home, he suddenly felt self-conscious. He worked hard because he wanted to, not because he had to. He'd never had to struggle financially.

He cleared his throat.

Jody glanced up. "Almost done." She stood and took all of three steps to reach the sink in the bathroom beside the closet. "You never answered me. Where do you live?" She grabbed a few items out of a drawer and snagged her toothbrush from a cup by the sink. "Well?"

"It's, ah, a bit larger than this place."

"I hope your house is huge. We'd be like sardines if we both had to stay here together."

Some of the tension went out of his shoulders. "Then it wouldn't bother you if I had a really big house with a few acres of land?"

"Tell me you have a million dollars in the bank and I'm yours forever."

"I have a million dollars in the bank. I guess we're getting married now."

She laughed and brushed past him to grab her bag. He reached to take it from her, and she rolled her eyes, moving it out of his reach. "You're on crutches. I can carry my own bag. Come on, Mr. Millionaire. I hope you have some New York strip or filet mignon in your freezer and a giant grill to cook them on."

He followed her to the front door, struggling to keep up since he wasn't used to crutches. When she reached to open the door, he said, "Hold it."

She glanced up at him expectantly.

"I do have steaks in the freezer."

She smiled. "Great."

"And a grill."

"Sounds perfect."

"And an outdoor kitchen."

"Okay."

"And a heated pool."

Her smile began to dim. "Any other deep confessions you want to make?"

"I really do have a million dollars in the bank. And then some."

She blinked, all signs of amusement gone. "That wasn't a joke?"

He slowly shook his head. "That wasn't a joke. Do you hate me now?"

She shoved her hair back from her face. "Look, I'm not prejudiced against rich people. Well, not *all* rich people. Just Amelia, Peter, Patricia, Patience, Patrick and Paul. I never mentioned that my estranged adoptive family is wealthy, did I?"

"No. You didn't. Your family has money but they don't share it with you?"

Shadows seemed to darken her eyes, just like they'd done up in the mountains when she'd mentioned her adoptive father.

"Jody?"

"It's…complicated. I don't want to talk about it."

"All right. Then, we're good? You don't mind going to my place?"

"We're good. Just as long as you don't live in Rutherford Estates. It's a ritzy development in the mountains outside of town where my real estate mogul adoptive father lives, along with my adoptive mom." She shivered dramatically. "It's like Mordor and the evil eye looking my way. That's why I'm over here in The Shire, making do with my little hobbit house." She grinned.

"Rutherford Estates?" He forced a laugh. "What would be the odds of your family and me living in the same area?"

"Exactly! Right? I shouldn't have even brought it up. Let's go."

JODY STOMPED PAST Adam into the foyer of his mansion—the one in Rutherford Estates—and didn't even spare him a glance. She was so angry she could spit. Seeing the expensive travertine floors spread out before her for miles made it even more tempting. She'd grown up in a place like this. And she had no desire to go back, or be within a few streets of where her family lived. He knew that and had brought her here anyway.

She clutched her bag and marched to the massive staircase just past the equally massive living area on the left side of the room, keeping her back turned to him. "I assume the bedrooms are upstairs. Which one is mine?"

Click. Click. The crutches sounded behind her as he approached. Part of her wanted to ignore him and run up the stairs, knowing he couldn't follow easily. The other part—the part she really hated right now—wanted to turn around and help him, ease him into one of the surprisingly cozy-looking leather chairs that sprinkled the room and get him a beer. Assuming he even had beer.

More likely he drank wine, something French with a hoity-toity label.

The clicks stopped.

"Jody?" As always with her, his deep voice was gentle and kind.

"I'm sorry," he said. "I should have told you where I lived when you asked me instead of tricking you into coming here. But there's an electrified fence around this property, motion sensors, alarms. This is the safest place I could think of to take you."

When she didn't reply, he said, "If you really want to, we can go. I'll call the limo driver back."

She clutched the banister. "Why are you always so nice to me?"

"You want me to be mean?"

She sighed and turned around. "Of course not."

"Okay." He looked thoroughly confused. "I'll book us a room in a nice hotel downtown. I can hire a security guy to watch the door—"

"Stop. Just stop. I'll stay here. And like you said, it's safe. I'll just have to do my best to forget that we're within walking distance of my evil adoptive dad." She forced a laugh and dropped her gaze to his chest.

His fingers gently tilted her chin up. His deep blue eyes searched hers. "I'm a good listener if you want to talk."

"I don't."

"If you change your mind—"

"I won't. Where's my room?"

His mouth tightened with disappointment. "There are four guest rooms upstairs, each with its own bathroom. Pick whichever one you like. My room is down here if you need me."

"Adam, I..."

"Yes?"

She shook her head. "Thank you. I mean it. You've done so much for me. I really appreciate it."

He nodded but didn't say anything.

She started up the stairs, then stopped and looked over her shoulder.

He hadn't moved. He was balancing on his crutches, watching her with an unreadable expression.

"You're not a real estate entrepreneur, are you?" she asked.

His brows raised. "If you're wondering where my money comes from, my great-great-grandfather was a business whiz and started a dozen companies. My parents gave ownership of some of those companies to my siblings and me as we each turned twenty-one."

Her face flushed with embarrassment. "I wasn't trying to find out how you got your money. I just... I'm glad you're not in real estate. That's all."

"Because of your adoptive father being in real estate?"

She swallowed, then nodded.

"But you don't want to talk about him?"

"I really don't. But...if I did...you would be the one I'd want to talk to." She gave him a watery smile, already struggling to hold back the tears that were threatening. "Good night, Adam."

"Good night, Jody."

She hurried up the rest of the stairs and went into

the first bedroom she found. After shutting the door, she slid down to the thick, plush carpet and drew her knees up to her chin. She wasn't going to get a wink of sleep knowing that the man she'd hated and feared all her life was just a short walk away. She couldn't tell Adam what Peter Ingram had done to her. She couldn't bear the revulsion that would cross his face. Or worse. She couldn't bear it if he turned out to be just like the rest of her adoptive family. She couldn't bear it if he didn't believe her.

She dropped her chin onto her knees and did what she'd done all her life when times got hard. She wept.

Chapter Seventeen

Jody hesitated at the top of the landing. She hadn't expected any lights to be on downstairs at two in the morning. She didn't want to intrude if Adam was still up, maybe watching a late movie or something.

Everything was quiet. And there were only a *few* lights on. Maybe he'd left them on for her, since she was in an unfamiliar house. He was like that. Nice. Kind. Considerate. Exactly the kind of man she'd always dreamed of, and exactly the kind of man she could never have because she was so dang screwed up.

She sighed and headed downstairs with no particular destination in mind. But she was going stir-crazy in her room, unable to sleep with so much rattling around in her brain. And her heart. Grief was a constant ache in her chest.

Figuring Adam wouldn't mind, she wandered through the sprawling house. It was refreshing to see that not everyone with money decorated their homes like a museum, the way her adoptive father decorated his.

The paintings here weren't modern atrocities of

splattered paint with no form or function, calling it-self art. Adam's paintings were comfortable, accessible, warm. His love of the outdoors was obvious in his choice of landscapes, most of them featuring mountains, lakes and ethereal forests that seemed so real she could swear she smelled the pine trees.

For such a big house, it didn't feel intimidating. She wasn't afraid that if she touched something it might break. She could easily see children running across the area rugs and bounding up the stairs, giggling and laughing and loving life—as all kids should.

She forced away the dark memories of her own child-hood that tried to press in on her and continued her ex-ploration. To the right of the foyer was a short hallway that she assumed led to Adam's bedroom. She paused, longing to go to him. Not because she *wanted* him, al-though she couldn't imagine ever *not* wanting him. To-night she *needed* him, needed someone to care about her, to hug her and hold her and tell her that she mat-tered. That would be selfish, though, waking him up just to give her a hug, no matter how deeply she craved his arms around her. So she forced herself to move past the hallway to the kitchen.

Of all the rooms in the house that she'd seen so far, this one was the most typical of what she'd expect in a place like this. He hadn't stamped his personality in here, his warmth. It was functional and beautiful, with cherry cabinets and black granite countertops. But there was nothing homey. It was too sterile, too impersonal, to be a reflection of him. Which made her doubt he used it much. Maybe he cooked out a lot in the outdoor kitchen that he'd mentioned earlier, or brought a lot of takeout food home.

Thinking of takeout had her tummy rumbling. She hadn't been hungry at the hospital and had only picked at the food on her plate. She had to search for the refrigerator and finally realized it was disguised with cabinet fronts to blend in with everything else.

Mission accomplished. It definitely blended.

Shaking her head, she opened the doors, then laughed. She pressed her hand to her mouth, belatedly hoping she hadn't been too loud. Then she rummaged through the containers of Chinese takeout, barbecue and leftover pizza. Most of the food still looked edible, and she was about to grab a slice of pepperoni pizza when she saw a plastic-wrapped plate sitting on the next shelf down. There was a note taped to the top.

Jody, just in case you wake up hungry, I cooked you a steak and grilled a potato. Wasn't sure how you like it, so I left the steak medium. —Adam

His thoughtfulness did funny things to her heart and of course had her eyes moist with tears. After all the tears she'd shed tonight, she hadn't expected that. She furiously wiped her eyes and then took out the plate. After warming it in the microwave and preparing the potato, she grabbed a beer—relieved to see he wasn't a wine drinker—and headed toward the dining room. Pausing at the entrance, she eyed the massive, lonely-looking table and changed directions, heading into the living room to the left of the stairs instead.

Now this room was exactly to her taste. Decorated in rich browns and golds, the furniture was plush leather with reclining seats. And a giant TV mounted over the fireplace. She set her beer in the cup holder on the big, cushy recliner that directly faced the TV, then settled down to eat her meal.

The first bite of steak melted in her mouth. She didn't think she'd ever had anything so good. Then again, she hadn't eaten a real meal in a few days, so that could have had something to do with it. She'd eaten half the potato and steak before she finally got full enough to slow down and leisurely enjoy the rest.

As she chewed, she glanced behind her to judge the distance between the living room and Adam's bedroom. She didn't think he'd hear her this far away, so she swiped the remote from the end table and clicked on the television. Just to make sure she didn't disturb him, she kept the volume low. Then she settled back to catch up on what had been happening in the world since she'd received that fateful text from Tracy's phone.

Since it was so late—or early, depending on how she wanted to look at it—local news wasn't an option. So she clicked on one of the twenty-four-hour national news channels. As usual, it was a kaleidoscope of unrest in the world, terrorist plots and political pundits offering so-called expert opinions based on hearsay and no firsthand knowledge. She was about to turn off the TV when one of the news anchors mentioned Gatlinburg.

Curious, she turned up the volume a couple of notches and leaned forward. Their little town was a tourist mecca. But other than the wildfires last season, nothing much happened around here to catch the attention of the national news shows.

Until now.

A picture of one of the local city councilmen, Eddie Hicks, flashed up on the screen. The anchor reminded the audience that Hicks had been killed in a car crash earlier in the week, the same day that Sam had gone missing.

Sam. Tracy. She missed them both so much.

The anchor gave details about the memorial service being held later today. Jody wasn't sure why that made the national news, until another picture flashed up on the screen —Tennessee state senator Ron Sinclair. He was well-known in Gatlinburg and heavily lauded for bringing several economy-boosting projects to town because of his work on an infrastructure subcommittee. Apparently, he was friends with the councilman and would be in town for the memorial. The mayor and other dignitaries would also be in attendance.

The anchor droned on about other events around the world as Jody finished her meal. Then she clicked off the TV and headed into the kitchen to clean up. After loading her plate and utensils in the dishwasher and making sure the kitchen was as pristine as she'd found it, she started toward the stairs again to go up to her room.

Then she noticed the pool through the back wall of French doors.

The water was a gorgeous cornflower blue, lit by lights from underneath. Since the homes around here were separated by several acres, none of them were close enough to have a view of the backyard. It was completely private and looked so peaceful and serene that it drew her forward like a magnet.

She started to open one of the doors, then stopped. There was an electronic keypad on the wall to the right. The security alarm. She hadn't even thought to ask Adam for the code. She pressed her face to the glass in frustration, then froze.

There was a man outside.

She stepped back, ready to run to Adam's room, then hesitated. The man's back was to her and he wasn't skulking around as if he was looking for a way into the house. He was sitting in one of the deck chairs facing the pool. As she watched, he turned his head to look down and picked up a bottle of beer she hadn't noticed before.

Adam.

She let out a shaky breath, relieved that Damien or one of his men hadn't found her. Then she frowned, noticing more details as her eyes adjusted to the dim light through the glass panes in the door. A holstered pistol sat on a small glass table beside his chair next to a legal pad. Dozens of balled-up pieces of paper lay discarded on the ground all around him. His phone was facedown on the concrete as if it had fallen from the table and he hadn't noticed.

What was going on? Why was he out there? Was his leg hurting so much that he couldn't sleep? That thought had her turning the knob and rushing outside.

"Adam, are you okay?" She hurried toward his chair. "Is your leg hurting too much to—" She stopped and blinked down at him. He didn't have a shirt on. He didn't have much of anything on. Actually, all he had on was his underwear—sexy boxer briefs that hugged all his…attributes…like a second skin.

Her mouth went dry as she stared at him, her gaze caressing every inch from his toes to his rippling abs to his lightly furred chest and, finally, up to eyes that reflected a deep blue in the light from the pool. But he wasn't looking at her. He was staring out at the darkness beyond the pool, his jaw clenched with agitation.

"Adam?"

He tipped the bottle of beer up to his lips and took a deep swig, emptying the bottle. Then he tossed it over his head into the pool. It landed with a splash and bobbed up and down before filling with water and slowly sinking beneath the surface.

Jody didn't have to look down into the pool to know the bottle he'd just emptied wasn't his first. And apparently it wasn't going to be his last, judging by the flush on his cheeks and the six-pack carton on the other side of his chair with one more bottle in it.

She put her hands on her hips. "You're drunk."

His eyes slowly rose to hers. "Not drunk enough." He picked up the other bottle and stared at it a moment, then squeezed his eyes shut as if in pain before throwing it unopened into the pool.

Jody lowered herself to her knees beside his chair. "Is it your leg?" She reached for his phone on the ground. "I can call the doctor, get him to phone in a stronger pain prescr—"

"I know about your adoptive father, Peter Ingram."

She went still, the phone clutched in her hand. "Excuse me?" she whispered.

His jaw clenched so tight the skin along his jawbone turned white. "The way you reacted when you mentioned him earlier, calling him your evil adoptive dad, how angry you were that I'd tricked you into coming here…" He scrubbed his face, covering his eyes with his hands before dropping them to his lap. "I know it was your story to tell. But I couldn't let it go. I had to know why you were so afraid of him." His tortured gaze finally rose to hers. "I'm so, so sorry."

"You had no right." Her voice came out a harsh croak. "You had no right."

"I know. Believe me, I know. I'm so sorry—"

"Stop saying that!" She jumped to her feet, finally finding her voice. "What are you sorry for anyway? Abusing your authority and opening a closed file you shouldn't have been able to open? That's what you had to have done. I was a juvenile. They sealed the record. No way could you have gotten that information without breaking a law or some kind of law enforcement code or something. Or are you sorry that you violated my privacy, violated *me* by prying into secrets that were mine to tell or not to tell?"

"Both. I shouldn't have pried, you're right. I abused your trust, my position as a federal officer. I never should have done it."

"No. You shouldn't have. I'm leaving, going back to my apartment. Don't bother driving me. You're too drunk to drive anyway. I'll call a cab." She turned and ran for the house.

"Jody, wait."

His chair creaked. She heard the click of his crutches as she threw open the door.

"Jody!"

She rushed inside.

A loud crack followed by the sound of shattering glass had her whirling around.

Adam lay on his back on the patio, his face twisted in agony as he clutched his hurt leg. His crutches had skittered out from beneath him and lay several feet away, right next to the shattered glass table that had been sitting beside his chair.

She ran back outside.

"No!" His voice was a hoarse whisper. "The glass. You'll get cut."

She stepped around the larger shards as she knelt beside him. "What can I do? How can I help? Are you cut?"

"Stop, Jody. You're barefoot."

"So are you. Can't you just accept help when you need it?" She grabbed his crutches, but when she tried to help him up, there was no way she could lift him. It took all her strength and a lot of cajoling and threatening to get him to even try to help her. Half-drunk Adam was ornery as all get-out and had an incredibly colorful vocabulary.

Finally she got him inside. Once they'd reached the living room, she was so exhausted she didn't even try to steer him down the hallway. Instead she jerked his crutches away and let him fall onto one of the mammoth couches.

He grunted when he landed, bounced a couple of times, then promptly passed out.

Jody's mouth dropped open in shock. Then she snapped it closed in anger. "Adam?" She grabbed his shoulder and shook him. "Adam?"

He started snoring.

She fisted her hands at her sides and kicked one of his crutches. It skittered across the room before spinning around and sliding halfway under a recliner. How dare he? How dare he invade her privacy, look into the most intimate details of her life without her permission, then not even stay awake long enough for her to yell at him? He should be begging her forgiveness and groveling at her feet.

She closed her eyes. Dang it. He *had* groveled. He *had* begged her forgiveness. And he'd nearly killed himself trying to chase after her because she'd refused to listen to him. She sagged down onto the couch beside him.

"Oh, Adam. What am I going to do with you?"

His soft snore was apparently the only answer she was going to get any time soon.

Obviously leaving him when he was passed out wasn't a good idea. Especially with his injured leg. Plus, she really didn't want to head out the front door with Damien possibly lurking around somewhere. All in all, she was pretty much a prisoner here for the time being. But come morning, when Adam was groaning with a headache over a cup of hot coffee, she'd make him take her back home. She had a gun. If Damien tried to come into her apartment, she'd gladly pull the trigger.

Adam's jaw tightened in his sleep, and his legs shifted restlessly. He reached toward his hurt leg, groaning, obviously in pain.

"You don't deserve my help, you know that, Adam?"

He winced and mumbled something incoherent but didn't wake up.

She shook her head and set about doing everything she could to ease his pain. Which basically amounted to straightening his leg, elevating it on a pillow and applying a cold compress that she'd found in his cavernous refrigerator. But it seemed to help, because he settled down and was no longer twitching in pain.

She sighed and raked a hand through her hair. A slight breeze had her realizing she'd left one of the French doors open. Outside the little pieces of crumpled-up paper still lay by Adam's chair. The broken table glass twinkled in the moonlight like a thousand little diamonds scattered across the concrete.

"A thousand little diamonds I get to sweep up," she grumbled.

Once again she trudged into the kitchen, locating the broom and dustpan in the pantry, exactly where it made sense they would be. Of course they were hanging on hooks, and what little food he had was lined up in neat rows on the shelves.

"I wonder if he folds his underwear, too." Her bin of underwear in her closet was a chaotic jumble. It would probably give him a heart attack. She grabbed a trash bag, conveniently on a shelf next to the broom, and headed outside.

The little table had obviously been made of safety

glass, probably the only reason she hadn't cut her feet when she ran outside. But even though the little pieces weren't wicked sharp, there were a lot of them. It took a good ten minutes before she was satisfied that she'd gotten up all the glass. She dumped the last of it into the garbage bag, then set about picking up the pieces of crumpled paper by Adam's chair.

Back inside, she set the legal pad and his phone on the counter and was about to stuff the garbage bag into the can under the sink when she noticed the writing on the pad. She grew still, then very slowly pulled the pad toward her and read the rest of it. By the time she'd read it all, tears were blurring her vision.

She hated that she was such a crier.

She wiped at her eyes, then slid to the floor and pulled the trash bag toward her. She picked out every piece of balled-up paper, unfolded them and smoothed them out so she could read them. Anyone else would probably be horrified at what he'd written. They might even call the police, thinking that he was dangerous. But Jody understood his anger, his fury and his desire for revenge better than anyone. And if she hadn't only known the man for a few days, she'd think she was half in love with him.

Because he was the only person, ever, who'd truly believed her.

The fact that she hadn't personally told him the details about the abuse she'd suffered at the hands of the man who'd adopted her didn't matter. Adam had read the police reports. He'd read the testimony in juvenile court. He'd read what the judge had decided, most likely after being given a substantial bribe by Jody's adoptive father. And still, Adam had believed her. That was what these pieces of paper told her. And to her they were a precious gift, something to treasure.

She carefully set each wrinkled piece of paper on the counter in a neat stack on top of the legal pad and threw the trash away. Then she headed into the family room. She set the pages on the end table, grabbed a blanket off the back of one of the chairs, then sat down beside Adam. She gently lifted his head and slipped closer, cradling his head on her lap. Then she covered both of them with the blanket and closed her eyes.

Chapter Eighteen

The smell of bacon had Adam bolting upright, then falling back with a groan. Pressing a hand to his throbbing head, he blinked up at the familiar coffered ceiling above him. Why was he on the couch? With a pillow beneath his head? And a blanket covering him? The last thing he remembered was sitting by the pool, nursing a beer to dull the pain in his leg, dreaming up all the different ways he could torture and kill Jody's adoptive father for what he'd done to her.

Jody. She'd been there, too. Hadn't she? There was an argument. Blinding pain as he'd fallen against…something. A loud crash. What in the world had happened?

He blinked his bleary eyes and forced himself to sit up. Then he looked over the end of the couch toward the kitchen, where the delicious—and nauseating, given his current state—smells were coming from.

Was she cooking breakfast? He could just catch a glimpse of her as she moved around inside the kitchen. Was she…humming?

She stuck her head around the corner. "About time you woke up. Breakfast will be ready in about ten minutes. Duncan will be here at nine to give us an update on the case. You should hurry up and get ready."

He blinked, certain he'd heard her wrong. "My brother? He called you?"

"Well, actually he called you." She picked up his phone off the island and held it up. "Hope you don't mind that I answered on your behalf." She motioned toward him. "There's a glass of water and some aspirin beside you, and something to settle your stomach if you need it." She looked over her shoulder. "The clock above your oven says you've used up one of your ten minutes. Chop, chop. I don't want your breakfast to get cold while you're dillydallying in the shower."

She disappeared into the kitchen.

Adam had a million questions for her, the most important being why she was so cheerful when he was pretty sure he'd been a moron and a jerk last night. But his roiling stomach, aching head and throbbing leg were taking center stage in his world at the moment. And they wouldn't be ignored.

He gratefully downed several aspirin, chasing them with a huge swig of Pepto and half a bottle of water.

"Six minutes," Jody called out from the kitchen, sounding disgustingly cheerful.

Was this the calm before the storm? Was she planning on poisoning him in return for whatever he'd done last night? He had a feeling he deserved it.

He grabbed the crutches she'd thoughtfully left on the floor beside the couch and hobbled his way into his bedroom. He tried to get ready quickly according to her timetable, but his attempts to shower without getting the bandage around his leg wet were a complete fiasco and he fell twice, finally giving up and just taking a normal shower—to hell with his stitches.

A few minutes later, feeling far more human than he should have thanks to the aspirin and Pepto, he made his way to the kitchen island.

The kitchen was empty.

"You're late."

He turned at the sound of her voice behind him. She was wearing curve-hugging blue jeans and an emerald-green button-up shirt that perfectly matched her eyes and her adorable glasses. Her gorgeous, thick red hair tumbled over her shoulders to hang halfway down her back. Just a touch of makeup made her eyes pop even more than usual. His mouth went dry just looking at her.

"You're beautiful," he breathed.

Her frown evaporated. "You're forgiven. Come on. Your plate's in the dining room."

He stood in confusion, but she seemed determined for him to eat and had gone to a lot of trouble, so he dutifully sat down. She'd made scrambled eggs, biscuits, bacon and hash browns. They were all expertly prepared. She was definitely talented in the kitchen. But in spite of how good everything tasted, he didn't want any of it. He wanted to talk instead, to beg her forgiveness for what little he remembered of his behavior last night, to rebuild the bridges he'd torn down. But she seemed so…happy…content to sit across from him. There were no recriminations on her tongue, no accusations, no tears.

That part bothered him the most.

He was used to her tears. He expected them. This smiling Jody without a seeming care in the world was an enigma. And he didn't know what to make of it.

When he'd finally eaten enough to feel that he wouldn't insult her if he stopped, he set his fork down. "You're a wonderful cook. You shouldn't have gone to all that trouble. But I appreciate it. Thank you."

She beamed at him. "You're very welcome." She took a sip of her orange juice.

"Jody?"

She looked at him over the rim of her glass, brows raised in question.

"Why are you doing this? Why did you cook me breakfast? And why are you being so sweet when I don't deserve any of this?"

She set the glass down and wiped her mouth with the napkin. "Wait here."

He started to ask her what she was talking about. But she hurried out of the room.

He clenched his fists on the table in frustration. He'd wanted to talk it out, see if they could move beyond last night. But she was putting up a front, not letting him in. Where had she gone? Was she upstairs, crying, after trying to be nice in spite of her hurt feelings? All alone? That thought had him pushing back his chair.

"No, please." She'd come back into the room. "Don't leave. We need to talk."

Now this he'd expected. He scooted his chair back under the table. "I know. I was a jerk last night. I abused my authority and—"

"Looked into my sealed juvenile records. Yes, I

know." She pulled a stack of wrinkled pages from behind her back and set them on the table.

Adam's stomach clenched. He was glad his appetite hadn't been what it normally was or he'd probably have thrown up right then and there.

"Do you know what these are?" She smoothed her hand over the top page.

He slowly nodded. "The ramblings of an idiot who drank far more than he should have. Jody, I had no right to—"

"No. You didn't. You shouldn't have gone behind my back and used your authority to find out details that were mine to share. Or not to share. I admit, when I realized what you'd done, I was furious, and hurt, and felt betrayed. I was ready to storm out of here."

"Why didn't you? Don't get me wrong. I'm glad you didn't. I'd have been worried about you and would have had to tear this town apart to find you. But why did you tuck me in on the couch and leave pills for my hangover and go to all that trouble to cook me breakfast? I should have been the one waiting on you, not the other way around. Why did you do all of that for me?"

She tapped the stack of pages on the table. "This. This is why I'm still here, why I'm not mad at you anymore." She held up the first page and squinted at it. "You have really bad penmanship, by the way."

"I was drunk."

"True, which means your inhibitions were lowered and you poured your emotions out onto these pages. Your true emotions, not subterfuge."

"Jody, I didn't mean for you to see—"

"'Castration,'" she read from the first page.

He choked and started coughing.

She looked at him over the top of her glasses and continued reading what he'd scribbled while under the influence of alcohol and an all-consuming rage.

"'Castration would be a good way to kill Jody's father. Bastards like that shouldn't be allowed to procreate.'"

She set the page to the side. "I agree. They shouldn't." She picked up the next page. "'Gunshot wound. Nothing quick or easy. I'd shoot him in the gut and tie him out in the sun to slowly and painfully bleed to death.'"

He cleared his throat again. "I'm actually not as bloodthirsty as I sound. I was just...fantasizing. I wouldn't *actually* do that to someone."

She picked up the next page. "'Caning. Maybe it's time that caning was brought to this country. I'd give cane poles to everyone who'd ever been abused by someone who'd sworn to love them and let them each have a turn at him until the lecherous light faded from his serpent's eyes.'"

"A bit melodramatic," he said, trying to smile as if he thought the whole thing was amusing. But he was pretty sure he failed spectacularly.

"This is a pretty good one." Her voice was tight. She cleared her throat and picked up the next paper, her hands slowly smoothing it out. "'I'd get one of my old buddies from the vice squad to plant seized child pornography pictures on his computer. Once in prison, the other inmates would enact their own form of punishment.'"

"I wouldn't really plant evidence."

"I'm sure you wouldn't," she agreed. She pulled another piece of paper from the very bottom of the stack. "This one is my personal favorite." The paper shook in her hands as she read. "'I'd tie him to a chair and, with his family watching—the vipers who turned their backs on Jody—I'd let her confront him about everything he did to her. I wouldn't let him go until he admitted what he'd done and begged for her forgiveness. And once her family realized they'd been wrong all this time, they'd beg her for forgiveness, too, and she could laugh in their faces. I'd take Jody away from those horrible, awful people and do everything I could to make her forget every bad thing that ever happened to her.'" Her chin wobbled as she read the last part of it. "I would *love* her."

Tears spilled over and ran down her cheeks.

He scooted his chair back, ready to go to her, but he hesitated. Was she angry or hurt or…what? He wasn't sure and didn't know what to do. How was he going to fix this?

"Thank you," she whispered brokenly.

"I'm sorry—what? You're…thanking me? Why?"

"You believed me. When no one else did. You have no idea what that did to me when I read those pages." She waved her hand in the air. "Oh, I know you would never actually do all of those things to Peter. But the fact that you believed in me enough to be that angry on my behalf goes a long way toward healing the holes in my heart." She stood and circled the table to stand in front of him. Then, to his shock, she straddled him in his chair.

He jerked against her, swearing, a bead of sweat popping out on his forehead as he grabbed her arms to lift her off him. "I don't think you're thinking straight. You should—"

She shoved his arms away and cupped his face in her hands. "I'm thinking with more clarity than I have in ages. And you were thinking more clearly when you wrote those pages than you realize. Your heart shined through in the concern you showed for me. And in that last sentence you wrote. I agree with you, Adam. Love really is the cure. Will you love me?"

"Sweetheart." He cleared his throat. "I mean... Jody—"

"I like *sweetheart* better." She pressed a soft kiss against his right cheek.

He shuddered and drew a ragged breath. "*Jody*, we've been through a traumatic few days together. Sometimes that makes people have, ah, feelings that might not prove to be real later on."

She kissed his other cheek, then shifted her bottom in a delightfully sinful way against his lap.

He grabbed the arms of the chair to keep from doing something he knew he would regret, like grabbing her. "Have *you* been drinking this morning?"

"Nope," she breathed against his neck. "I'm stone-cold sober. Love me, Adam."

He grasped her arms and pulled her against him, then swore when he realized what he was doing. He gently pushed her back against the table. "Be careful. My control is hanging by a thread here. I'm trying to do the honorable thing."

She let out a deep sigh and scooted farther back on his thighs but didn't get up. "I don't know why you think making love to me isn't honorable. It would be two consenting adults who care about each other and want to show their feelings in the most wonderful way possible."

He started to protest her warped view of honorable, but she shook her head and held a finger to his lips.

"Knowing you, I imagine that you're worried I'm vulnerable. But I've never felt so empowered in my life. By believing in me, you've helped me feel less hopeless, more in control, than I have in years. Thank you for that."

He cleared his throat. "Um. You're welcome?"

She smiled, then took his hands in hers. "My parents, my biological parents, were killed in a car wreck when I was a toddler. I barely remember them. Mostly I just know their names—Lance and Vanessa Radcliffe— and that they loved me enough to make sure that I was taken care of when they died. Or at least, that's what they thought—that I'd be well taken care of because of everything they put into place, like designating their best friends, the Ingrams, as my guardians."

"Jody, you don't have to tell me any of this."

"I know. And that's why I want to, because I don't have to. And because…because I've never told anyone the whole story. Not even the judge who oversaw the hearing against Peter Ingram. Not even the prosecutor who pressed the case. Not even Tracy. She knew bits and pieces, but no one knows it all. Except me."

She shoved her hair back from her face and drew a deep breath. "After my parents were killed, the Ingrams took me in, eventually adopted me. Everyone thought they were being good Samaritans, honoring their friends. But they never really wanted me. They wanted the Radcliffe family home here in Rutherford Estates that came with me, and my trust fund. The house has its own trust fund just for its upkeep and taxes, to ensure that I'd never have to worry about having a home."

Adam frowned. "But you live in an apartment. Shouldn't the house be yours now that you're a legal adult?"

She shrugged. "You would think so. The Ingrams showed me the deed and a copy of my parents' will giving them ownership in exchange for taking care of me. I guess my biological parents thought the trust fund they set up for me would be enough once I was out on my own, that I could buy my own house at that point."

"It wasn't enough?"

Her mouth tightened. "It should have been. But the Ingrams made large withdrawals against the fund while I was growing up, supposedly for my care. There was barely enough to get me through college when I came into ownership of the fund and they lost control of it." She held her hand up. "And before you ask, yes, I petitioned the court for an accounting of their stewardship, hoping I could force them to pay back some of the money. But after an accountant reviewed the records, a judge ruled that they hadn't done anything illegal. I could have appealed, but I decided to let it drop at that point."

Adam didn't like what he was hearing. It sounded

fishy to him. Maybe he could look into it sometime, if she wanted him to. But it wasn't the financial misdeeds of the Ingrams—if indeed they had done anything illegal—that worried him right now. It was the way Jody had turned pale as she prepared to tell him the details about her childhood.

He didn't want to know any more than what he'd read in the court transcripts.

The house she'd grown up in was just a few blocks away. He knew because he'd looked it up when he'd looked into her background. He already cared deeply about her. How was he supposed to sit here and not run over there and kill the man who'd hurt her? He was afraid of what he might do if she told him in her own words what her adoptive father had done to her.

He was about to remind her again that she didn't need to tell him any of the details. But she was staring at him, her green eyes searching his with a mixture of trust, and hope, and fear. And he knew he couldn't tell her no. She wanted this, needed this, needed to share with him what had happened to her. And he was in awe that it was him she trusted to share it with. So even though it almost killed him, he endeavored to listen and be there for her, and to not go kill Peter Ingram once she was finished.

He drew her against his chest.

She clung to him for several minutes, then relaxed. "The first time he came into my room at night, when everyone else in the house was asleep, I was nine."

Dear God. He closed his eyes and spent the next twenty minutes in agony listening to the harrowing details of her abuse. He remembered, in the mountains, thinking about how young she was, and that she was naive, inexperienced and sheltered in the horrors that existed in the world around her. What a fool he'd been. She was none of those things. She'd suffered horrendous abuse and learned about the ugliness that existed in this world far sooner than she ever should have. He felt like such an idiot for judging her, making assumptions. And now, as he sat here, listening to what had happened to her, all he wanted to do was grab his gun and storm out of the house. He wanted to kill the man who'd hurt her. If Jody wasn't nestled in his arms right now, so trusting and needing him in this moment, he very well might have. He stayed, for her, but it tore him up inside.

The abuse she'd suffered was horrific, far worse than anything listed in the court records. He didn't know how she'd managed to survive and become the well-adjusted, caring, kind person that she was today. She'd been abused by her adoptive father. And then abused again, betrayed, victimized by every member of her supposed family when they took their father's side against her after she finally told a counselor at school what was going on.

And if that wasn't enough, the social worker in the case and the court-appointed psychiatrist took the father's side as well. They claimed that Jody was lying, acting out, wanting attention. And when the proceedings were over, they found the father innocent and forced Jody to attend psychiatric sessions for years—

to work on her issues with being needy and attention seeking and being a pathological liar.

And they sent her back to live with her abuser and his family.

As far as Adam was concerned, all of them—her adoptive father, his family, the judge, the psychiatrist, the social worker—should have gone to prison, lost their jobs and anything else that could be legally done to punish them for failing to protect the innocent little girl entrusted to their care.

"After that," she continued, whispering against his chest, "I was treated like a servant, like Cinderella, doing all the chores, eating alone, being pulled out of my school and sent off to the bad kids' school. It was as if I didn't exist to them anymore. I was invisible and I didn't matter. The only good thing was that Peter never touched me again. I think he was worried that his wife was suspicious, that maybe she believed me but wouldn't go against him. The only reason I think that is because the day after the judge made his ruling, a steel bolt showed up on my door. I could bar it from the inside and there wasn't any way to unlock it from the hallway. No one ever said who put it there. No one even mentioned it. But I think it was my adoptive mom. Whoever did it, that bolt was the only thing that kept me sane, gave me hope that one day maybe things would get better."

She sat back and brushed at the tears on her cheeks. "I think I would have died of loneliness and despair if it hadn't been for Tracy and her family. I began spending more and more time with them, until I rarely ever went home. My family didn't care, of course, as long as the trust fund checks kept coming in every month. The moment I turned eighteen, I was out of there. And I've never been back."

She let out a shuddering breath. "Tracy and her family loved me and supported me, but even they were skeptical. It was the one wound in my heart where they were concerned. My family, and the experts, had painted such a terrible picture of me that even Tracy believed I was damaged, maybe traumatized from losing my biological parents at such a young age and that I was an attention seeker."

"How could you have stayed friends with her after that?"

She shrugged. "That's life. It's how it's always been. No one truly believed everything that I said happened. Until you. Why, Adam? Why did you believe me when no one else did?"

"Because I know you, know what's in your heart. We've been through more together in a few days than most people survive in a lifetime. I've seen the good in you, the kindness, the honesty. Why would I doubt you?" He opened his arms, and she fell against him.

It didn't surprise him when she began weeping. If anything, it was reassuring. Crying was her way of coping. She'd just relived her horrible ordeal by saying it out loud to him. The copious tears meant that she'd be okay. Or as okay as she could be with everything she'd been through.

When she started hiccupping, she pulled back. "I'm so sorry. I cry at the drop of a hat. It must be incredibly annoying."

"Not at all. It's part of who you are. It shows you're sensitive and have a wonderful, full heart in spite of everything that's happened to you. It would break my heart if you ever stop having that capacity to care and feel so deeply that you *don't* cry. Don't ever apologize for feeling and being honest about your emotions."

She lay back against him, her arms around his waist. He rested his chin on the top of her head and gently stroked her back. They sat that way for a long time, until the air around them seemed to subtly change. Her fingers curled against his shirt. Her breathing turned ragged. She slowly slid her hands up his chest and entwined her arms around his neck.

"Adam."

Just one whispered word, said with such a mixture of longing and desire, was all it took to send a jolt of raw lust straight through his body.

Then she pressed her open mouth against his neck and lightly touched her tongue to his overheated skin.

He almost came right out of his chair.

His hands tightened around her, trying to stop her wandering mouth. "Jody," he rasped. "Don't."

She kissed him again.

"Jody, no. Stop. You're vulnerable, emotional. You'll regret this later if you—"

She moved to his ear, her tongue doing wicked things that had him hardening in an instant.

He shuddered, his arms tightening around her, drawing her close. *No!* What was he doing? This was wrong. He couldn't act on the chemistry that flared between them every time they were close. Not now, not like this.

"Jody, you're not thinking clearly. You're not—"

She pressed her mouth against his neck and sucked. He jerked back.

She pulled back and stared up at him and ran her fingers through the hair at the nape of his neck. "I want you Adam. I need you."

"You'll hate me later. When you're thinking more clearly, you'll realize that—"

"Do you want me?"

He swallowed, hard. "You know I do."

"Then love me." She didn't wait for his response. She pulled him down to her and kissed his mouth.

He should have been stronger. Should have set her away from him. But he wanted her so badly he ached. There was something about this beautiful, smart, incredibly sweet woman in his arms that turned his knees to jelly. By the time her tongue darted inside his mouth and stroked his, he was already waving the white flag of surrender. He couldn't have stopped now if a whole army was at his door, trying to break it down. For some reason she needed him. And he needed her just as desperately.

He broke the kiss and gasped for air. Then leaned in and tortured her the same way she'd tortured him earlier. He pressed his mouth against her neck and sucked.

She gasped and almost overturned the chair.

He laughed and pulled back, his mouth hovering inches from hers. "What time did you say Duncan would be here?"

She swallowed, with obvious difficulty. "N…nine o'clock… I think."

He looked past her to the digital readout over the oven. "That's not nearly enough time."

"We'll make it work!" She jumped off his lap, grabbing the table to keep from falling when she tripped over her own feet. She picked up his crutches. "Hurry." She shoved them into his hands and took off down the hall, her bare feet slapping against the tile.

Adam was laughing so hard he could barely keep the crutches under his arms as he followed her to the bedroom at his aggravatingly much slower pace.

Chapter Nineteen

Jody stood naked in the middle of Adam's bedroom, her clothes discarded in a pile at her feet. The *click, click* of his crutches echoed through the house beyond the bedroom door as he slowly made his way toward her. And even though she'd had the occasional tryst in college and had always wanted them this way—fast, furious, two sweaty bodies seeking quick solace before she shoved the man of the hour out the door—suddenly everything about this seemed wrong.

Because this was Adam.

He wasn't like the men who'd drifted in and out of her life. Men who, according to her college counselors when she'd sought therapy on her own, were Jody's way of taking control of her body, in response to the abuse she'd suffered as a child when she'd been completely helpless to stop it. But Adam was different, special. Shouldn't that make…this…different? She looked down at her clothes, her naked body, and suddenly felt shy, nervous.

Click. Click.

She lunged for the chair by the bed and grabbed the blanket off the back.

The door opened behind her.

She spun around, clutching the blanket against her breasts, quickly shaking it out to cover more of her naked skin.

Adam stopped in the doorway, leaning heavily on his crutches, his face pale, eyes wide as they swept her from head to toe. "What's wrong? Second thoughts?"

"What?" She looked down at the blanket, clutched like a lifeline in her hands. "Oh. No, no, of course not. It's just that…" She looked up at him again, took a step toward him. "Are you okay? You look like you're in pain."

"And you look scared. Jody, it's all right. We don't have to do this. I'll just go back—"

"No!" She hurried to him, stopping a few feet away. "It's just…nerves. It's been a while, since college." She took off her glasses and tossed them onto her pile of clothes. "I'm not scared. I could never be afraid of you, Adam. I want you, very much. Don't you want me?" She dropped the blanket.

His gaze dipped. His throat worked. "You have no idea how badly I want you." His voice was thick with desire.

Feeling more confident now, she smiled and slipped into the role she'd always taken with these encounters. She put her hand on his arm and led him toward the bed. Then she shoved the covers back and lay down. She lifted her heavy fall of hair and fanned it out on the pillow, then held her arms up for him to join her.

Some of the heat seemed to leave his eyes as he stared down at her.

She suddenly felt self-conscious again. "Adam? What's wrong? Don't you like the way I look?" Men always did. They loved her thick red hair, her narrow waist, her curvy hips. Her breasts weren't as large as she would have preferred. But they were firm and well shaped. No one had ever had any complaints. "Adam?"

He swallowed again, his knuckles whitening where he was holding on to the crutches. "I think you're the most beautiful creature I've ever seen. And I want you, more than you could possibly imagine. But I want you to want me, too, really want me."

She frowned. "I do. I'm here, aren't I? I'm ready. Let's do it."

He winced. "You make it sound like a chore."

Her face flushed with heat, and she curled her fingers into the sheets. "Well if it is, I'm good at it. No one's ever said otherwise." She grabbed for the covers, pulling them up to her neck. "I don't understand you. We're both adults. We want each other. We should be rolling in the sheets right now, halfway done."

"Halfway *done*? Oh, sweetheart. It would take a lifetime for me to love you the way I want to, the way you deserve to be loved. I assure you we wouldn't be *halfway done* by now."

She frowned in confusion. "Are we going to have sex or not?"

The mattress dipped as he sat beside her. "No. We are not going to *have sex*."

She crossed her arms and stared up at the ceiling.

"We're going to make love. If you want to."

She turned her head on the pillow to look at him. "What's the difference?"

He smiled sadly. "Everything." He reached for her hand.

Aggravated, frustrated, she resisted, keeping her fingers curled into her palm.

He didn't try to uncurl her fingers. Instead, he leaned down and pressed an achingly soft kiss against the back of her wrist. Her skin heated beneath his touch. He moved his mouth along her thumb, kissing, caressing.

Raw pleasure zinged straight to her core.

She drew a ragged breath, fascinated as she watched his long lashes form crescents against his cheeks when he closed his eyes and bent over her arm. The incredibly erotic treatment continued. He worshipped her skin with his mouth, his tongue blazing a trail of lava everywhere he touched. She uncurled her fingers, curious what else he might do. He pulled one of them into his mouth…and sucked.

She jerked against the mattress, her other hand curling into the sheets. Heat unfurled in her belly. Every muscle tightened. Her pulse leaped, her breaths ragged.

And he was only kissing her hand.

He raised his head, breaking contact with her skin. She almost whimpered at the loss of his heat.

"Do you want me to stop?" he whispered.

"Hell no," she gasped.

His mouth curved into a hungry smile that *did* have her whimpering this time. She shifted her legs restlessly against each other and held her arms out to him.

But he didn't climb on top of her. Instead, he lowered his mouth to her elbow.

The man seemed to know where every nerve ending in her body was located. He massaged, caressed and kissed her into a frenzy. When he moved to her inner thigh, she came off the mattress, bucking against him.

Still, he refused to hurry, to take what he wanted from her, to slake his body in hers as others had done. The realization shot through her. With others, she'd had sex. This, this was what making love was about. Giving, not taking. Cherishing, gifting her with his body instead of making demands. She'd never experienced anything so incredible, so sweet, so beautiful.

"Jody? Sweetheart? Are you okay?" His breath fanned out across her thigh as he looked up at her.

She realized she was crying. Again. She swiped at the tears. "I'm more than okay. I'm in awe."

"Good tears, then?"

She drew a ragged breath. "Good tears. Um, you're not going to stop yet, are you?"

He grinned and slowly shook his head. "We're a long way from done." Then he lowered his head and flicked her core with his tongue.

"Adam!"

Where before he'd been gentle, slow, tender, now he was a demanding lover, ruthless in wringing every ounce of pleasure from her that he could. She thrashed against the bed, her hands threaded in his hair as her climax exploded through her. Still he kissed her, stroked her, drawing it out until colors burst behind her eyelids and her toes curled against the bed.

She heard the familiar sound of a foil packet being ripped open, felt the bed dip and knew he was protecting her. Then, finally, he moved up her body, fitting himself to her. She was limp, spent, but the feel of him hard and thick against her sent a jolt of heat straight through her. She dragged his lips to hers and lifted her legs, wrapping them around his waist, inviting him in.

This time, he didn't hesitate. He claimed her mouth and her body at the same time, thrusting into her. His hands moved between them, doing wicked things, building the pressure again, spiraling her up to even greater heights. He filled her so completely, so perfectly, his body fitting to hers like they were made for each other. She'd never felt such pleasure, such completeness, such joy before. As if this was meant to be. Destiny. Fate.

She felt him tighten inside her, knew he was close. But her ever-considerate lover placed her needs above his own once again, holding back, caressing, kissing, molding her body with his hands until she was again at those lofty heights, on the brink. Then he thrust into her again, sending them both tumbling over the edge. She cried out in wonder, clasping him to her as they both shattered into pieces and then slowly drifted back down to earth. Together.

Chapter Twenty

Duncan set his coffee down on the dining room table and glanced back and forth between Jody and Adam. "Am I missing something? Both of you are yawning like there's no tomorrow. You're either sleepy or you're worn-out. What have you been doing?"

Jody choked.

Adam coughed, then cleared his throat. Jody was so red with embarrassment that he wanted to grin. But he didn't dare. She'd probably murder him if he did.

"You have new information about the investigation?" he asked his brother.

When Jody wasn't looking, Duncan grinned and winked at Adam, letting him know he knew full well what they'd been doing.

Adam narrowed his eyes in warning. What he'd shared with Jody had been life changing. No way was he going to let his brother's juvenile teasing cheapen it in any way, for either of them.

He gave Jody an apologetic smile. It had been like a bucket of cold water having to hurry and wash and dress before his brother got there. Both of them had wanted to lie in bed all day, exploring the newfound closeness between them. But life wouldn't let them. Cold reality had intruded all too soon. He hadn't even gotten a chance to talk to her about what had happened between them, and whether her heart was as tangled up in the experience as his.

They'd only met a few days ago. But he already couldn't imagine his life without her in it somehow. Did she feel the same way? He desperately wanted to know. Instead, he was stuck here at his dining room table with his brother sitting across from him.

"Why are you frowning at me?" Duncan teased. "Did you wake up on the wrong side of the bed or something?"

"Or something," Adam gritted out, belatedly wishing he'd called his brother and told him not to come over at all. But that would have been selfish. Jody's safety rested on Duncan solving the case. Everything else, no matter how pleasurable, needed to come second.

"Just tell us what updates you have."

Duncan set his briefcase on the dining room table and popped it open. "Saying I have updates is stretching it. For as many threads as we have on this thing, they're unraveling far too slowly and not really leading anywhere."

He took out several folders and plopped them onto the table, then snapped his briefcase closed and set it on the floor. "These are the five cases Sam seemed to be focused on the most in the week before he was killed." He winced. "Sorry, Jody. I should have led with that, with a lot more finesse. The coroner confirmed a body we found was Sam. I'm very sorry for your loss."

She blinked and shook her head as if to clear it. She appeared to be having as much trouble as Adam focusing on the case. "It's okay. I mean, it's not okay. But I'd pretty much accepted that he had to be, that he was gone. To hear you confirm it isn't a shock at this point. It's just sad, and so unfair." She waved toward the folders. "Please, continue."

Adam wanted to pull her onto his lap and hold her, comfort her. But he didn't know how she'd feel about that in front of his brother. Damn it. They needed to talk, privately.

"Like I said, these are the five cases we determined that he was actively working. All of them have stacks of photographs in them."

Adam let out a deep breath and resolved to pay attention, no matter how difficult. He pulled one of the folders toward him and flipped through the small stack of pictures. "I'm not noticing any gaps in time stamps in this one."

Jody pulled another one of the folders toward her and opened it.

"There aren't any gaps in *any* of them," Duncan said.

She frowned. "No gaps?"

"None. We looked in all of the other case folders, too. Like you said, your boss was very detail oriented. Each case has an index listing the pictures that should be there. Everything matches up. We've hit a dead end."

Adam shook his head. "No. You haven't. You've learned something important."

Duncan arched a brow in question, and Jody looked at him, both waiting.

"You've learned that whatever Damien is after isn't related to any cases that Sam was officially working on."

Duncan stared at him intently. Then he sat back in his chair. "You should be an investigator, Adam. That makes complete sense. We've been looking at this all wrong. Sam must have been investigating something else, on his own. Not for a client. That would explain the gap. If he was working something on the side, he'd have no reason to keep the information at his office with his regular cases. He'd put it somewhere else. I would think it would be at his home, so he could keep it separate from regular work. But we searched there, found nothing." He shook his head. "We're still at an impasse. I'm not sure where to go with this. But I'll update the guy working on it. Maybe he can find a thread I haven't thought of."

"Guy? Not guys, plural?" Adam rested his forearms on the table. "What's going on? I thought you had a whole team working on this."

"Yeah, well, I did. We want justice for Mr. Campbell and Miss Larson. And we want to get Damien and Ned and anyone else who may be involved off the streets and locked up where they belong. But, well, resources being what they are, the guys higher up than me make executive decisions based on budget and higher priorities."

Adam swore. "What's a higher priority than making sure Jody isn't murdered? I thought the press had wind of this case and was putting pressure on you to solve it?"

Jody put her hand on his. "Please. Don't fight over me. I'll be okay."

He laced their fingers together. Even with her life on the line, she focused on others, on him. After what she'd suffered in her life, it was a miracle that she wasn't bitter and angry all the time. Instead she was selfless and sweet. He squeezed her hand in his.

"You *will* be okay," he said. "Because I'm not going to let anything happen to you. But you shouldn't have to live in fear wondering when Damien might try to strike. We need to end this. And that means the government needs to put its resources back on the case." He shot his brother an accusing look. "What are you working on if not this?"

"Something that's being kept hush-hush right now. I'm not at liberty to discuss it."

Adam leaned forward. "I'd expect that from Ian, not from you. Spill. Tell me what's going on."

"Who's Ian?" Jody asked.

Duncan gave her an apologetic smile. "Sorry. Ian is our youngest brother. He's always been a bit, well, rebellious. Doesn't exactly get along with the rest of us on the rare occasions that we even see him."

"Us? Just how big is your family?" she asked.

Duncan turned an accusing look at Adam. "Were you in too much of a hurry to even go through the niceties first?"

Jody's brows drew together in obvious confusion. But Adam wasn't confused in the least. His brother was berating him for making love to Jody without the two of them really getting to know each other first. And he had every right to shame him. Jody deserved better, and he hadn't bothered to share anything substantive about himself with her even though she'd shared the most intimate details of her life with him.

"I'm sorry I didn't tell you more about myself or my family," Adam said. "Really short version for now, I have three brothers—Duncan, Colin and Ian. My dad, William, is a retired federal judge. Margaret, my mom, is a retired prosecutor and—"

"Wait, Judge William McKenzie? I should have made the connection earlier. You're a part of the infamous Mighty McKenzies, aren't you? Your family's a legend at the courthouse. Every member is in law-enforcement in one way or the other, right?"

He winced. "We're not fans of that label. But yes, that's us. Except for Ian. But that's not important right now. The point, that we need to get back to, is that Duncan should be working this case with a full team of investigators. And he's not leaving until he tells us what so-called higher priority trumps protecting you by finding the guys who are trying to hurt you."

This time it was Duncan's turn to look uncomfortable. "I wouldn't put it that way exactly." He held up his hand to stop Adam. "But I'll remind you that I don't set the priorities. I didn't want to tell you what I was working on because I knew it would only upset you even more."

"Duncan—"

"But I'll tell you anyway. Eddie Hicks, a local city councilman, was murdered last week. Turns out he was assisting Senator Sinclair with some local research for an infrastructure bill that was passed by Congress a few days ago after pending in subcommittee for well over a year."

"Infrastructure?" Adam asked. "I vaguely remember seeing something about that on the news. Wasn't the government looking into buying up all the land associated with it?"

Duncan nodded. "A highway and bridge bill. This local councilman has been assisting Sinclair with surveys and research on the tracts of land involved, title searches and things like that. Getting appraisals and, as you said, buying up the land in preparation for the passage of the bill." He idly straightened the folders sitting on the table. "Sinclair and Hicks were apparently good friends."

Adam clenched a fist on the table. "So the senator is using his power to push the National Park Service and everyone else to steer their resources toward finding out who killed his friend instead of protecting Jody. Our taxpayer dollars at work. Nepotism is alive and well."

Duncan shoved back from the table and stood. "Like I said, I knew you'd be upset. I argued against this. In the end there was nothing I could do. I was fortunate just to get them to agree to leave one investigator assigned to the case." He set a business card on the table. "Here's his contact information, Jody, if you think of anything else that might help. I'll check back in with him as often as I can to ensure he keeps at it. And as soon as the councilman's case is resolved, I'll push to get more resources reassigned to your case." He spread his hands out beside him. "I'm really sorry. It's out of my control." He turned and headed toward the front door.

Adam followed, clicking after him on his crutches. In the opening, he let out an exasperated breath. "I'm sorry I'm taking my anger out on you, Duncan. I know none of this is your fault."

His brother gave him a sympathetic look. "You care about her."

"Well, of course I care about her." He kept his voice low, even though he doubted that Jody could hear him back in the dining room. "She's a good person. She doesn't deserve any of what's happening to her. I want Damien and whoever put him up to this found before she gets hurt."

"I know. I'm doing everything I can to help, officially and unofficially. In the meantime, just keep watching over her. And don't hesitate to call me if you need me. No matter what."

"I will. Did you mean to leave those folders?"

"They're copies. I don't think you'll find anything useful in them. But it couldn't hurt to have another pair of eyes on the case. I told the lone remaining investigator to email you if he found anything else significant."

"Thanks. I know that's against the rules. I appreciate it."

Duncan bumped him on the shoulder, his version of a hug, then headed outside.

Adam shut the door and leaned back against it. He was furious with the government for letting politics decide their priorities. But he also knew his brother well, and he knew that Duncan would have already done everything possible to change their minds. Since Duncan hadn't been successful, Adam needed to pick up where the government had left off. He was effectively on leave until his leg healed anyway. Might as well use that time to do what the government should have been doing—solving the case.

He headed to the table, his crutches making a tapping sound on the tile that drove him to distraction. When he stopped beside Jody's chair, she looked up at him in question. He wanted to kiss her so badly right now. But he knew where that would end. And his desire to make her safe outweighed everything else at the moment.

"Pretend you're Sam Campbell."

She blinked. "What? Why?"

"You knew him pretty well, right? Think like him. Tell me about his daily routine."

"I already told Duncan, during the chopper flight to the hospital—"

"I was a bit out of it during that flight. Tell me what you told him."

"Okay. I'll try."

He pulled out the chair beside her and listened to her tell him about her boss. He could see the love and admiration she felt for him. And it broke his heart that she'd suffered two devastating losses of people close to her in a handful of days. But what mattered the most was making sure that she didn't become victim number three.

"Okay," he said, when she finished talking about Sam. "What I'm hearing is he had a regimented schedule and documented everything. Other than when his grief for his wife overcame him, he never veered from that routine. So if he was working a secret case in the week before he died, he would have documented it just like everything else, right?"

"Right. Makes sense."

"But he didn't keep the documents at the office."

"Agreed. But I still don't know where he would have put them."

He tapped the table as he thought some more. "Did he seem afraid before he disappeared?"

"No. Not at all."

"Did he do anything different, out of the ordinary? Anything at all that you noticed?"

She started to shake her head, then stopped. "Well, it seems silly, really. I'm sure it's not related."

"Let me be the judge of that."

"A few days before he disappeared, he was extra nice to me. Not that he wasn't always nice. But he did more things with me than usual. I was his assistant, so usually he worked a case and I was his gofer, running errands for him. But that last week, just a few times, it was like he was *my* assistant instead. I remember it was the anniversary of his wife's death that week, and I attributed it to him being lonely."

"Be specific, Jody. What did he do?"

She thought about it a moment. "He talked to me, in the car, about my family, both my birth parents and my adoptive ones. It was awkward because I never tell anyone about them, or what happened. So it was a short conversation. I certainly didn't tell him about the abuse. He had lunch with me two or three times, asking more questions, like he was just trying to get to know me better. Oh, and one night, after work, he knew I was going to my storage unit and he said he'd like to see what I do when I'm not working for him. He seemed so lonely, so I let him come along."

"Did he give Tracy any extra attention that week?"

She shook her head. "I don't think so. Not that I recall."

"What kinds of questions did he ask you about your family?"

"The usual—whether I had brothers and sisters, where I grew up. I told him I was adopted, that my biological parents were killed in a crash. I remember he asked my birth parents' names, but after that he dropped the questions. I think he could tell I was uncomfortable and he changed the subject."

Adam shoved back from his chair. "Where's that storage unit of yours located?"

"In the middle of nowhere—not far from here, actually. We passed it on the way to your house last night. It's in the last flat section in the valley right before you climb into these foothills. Why?"

He held out his hand toward her. "We're going to take a little trip. If I'm right, we'll find the evidence that Damien was looking for hidden in your storage unit."

She took his hand and slowly stood. "You think Sam was working on a secret investigation and that he put something in my storage unit to hide it? Why would he do that?"

"I don't know. But it's the only place that makes sense, given your accounting of what he did that last week."

"Wait." She tugged her hand from his. "I'm getting my gun. It's in my room."

He tapped the holster on his hip. "I've got mine. It's my job to protect you."

"And it's my job to protect you."

She turned away before he could argue and headed up the stairs.

Chapter Twenty-One

Jody rubbed her hands up and down her arms. On the other side of the small table in the middle of her storage unit, Adam sat flipping through the folder they'd found.

"I can't believe Sam snuck that in here, or that he hid it in a pile of my photographs. Why would he do that?"

Adam didn't answer. She wasn't even sure that he'd heard her. He seemed engrossed in whatever he was reading.

"Adam?"

"Hmm?"

She sighed and glanced over her shoulder at the opening. The rolling door was down. Adam was so worried about keeping her safe that he'd insisted on keeping them locked inside while they searched the place. She never usually shut the door when she was here. It was too much like a cave. Or a prison.

Or her room back home, when she'd watched a similar slit beneath her door and prayed she wouldn't hear footsteps in the hallway.

She swallowed and turned back toward Adam. He was frowning down at a piece of paper.

"More title searches and real estate transactions?" she asked.

"Pretty much. And bills of sale. I'm no expert on that infrastructure bill Duncan mentioned earlier in relation to that city councilman and Senator Sinclair. But I remember a few local news reports about the government buying up land for right of way." He lifted his gaze to hers. "A lot of these tracts of land mentioned in these bills of sale are ones from the news reports. The buyer is the government. The seller on most of these is a company named Preferred Parcel Purchasing Corporation. That's a lot of P's. Remind you of anyone connected to you?"

Her pulse leaped in her throat. "Peter, Patricia, Patience, Patrick, Paul. You think my adoptive father set up a shell company? And that he's involved in some kind of crooked real estate deals that Sam discovered?"

"We've already established that Peter Ingram is a lowlife. Connecting the dots to shady business deals isn't much of a stretch. Another company listed on some of these transactions is Amelia Enterprises. Isn't your adoptive mother's name Amelia?"

She nodded, her entire body flushing hot and cold. She'd always thought of her adoptive father as evil. But could he be evil enough to have had someone kill Sam and Tracy? Was he trying to have her killed, too? Because of land deals? And money?

"I don't understand," she said. "He's wealthy. There's no reason for him to do anything illegal to get more money."

"Maybe Peter isn't as well-off as you think. Bad

investments, a struggling economy, poor decisions—
they can quickly ruin someone financially. If he's had
heavy losses, he might be desperate enough to make
deals with some pretty bad people—like Damien Flint."
He held one of the documents up and pointed to a bold
signature scrawled across the bottom. "The witness on
all of these documents is Judge Martin Jackson. Ever
heard of him?"

Something about the name sent butterflies loose in
her stomach. "I'm not sure. It sounds familiar. But it's
not an uncommon name."

"Maybe." He didn't sound convinced. "I know I've
seen it somewhere recently." He flipped the folder
closed. "It will come to me. In the meantime, I think
we should head back to my house. I'll tell Duncan what
we've found and have him send someone for this folder.
He'll want to search the rest of the storage unit." His
jaw tightened. "When he has resources. Is that okay
with you?"

"Of course. If it helps with the case, by all means.
Did you find anything in the folder to explain why
someone would want to hurt Sam? Or Tracy?"

"Or you?"

She swallowed. "Or me."

"I haven't found a connection yet. But I will. Or
Duncan will. Don't worry, Jody. I'll take care of you."

"I'll take care of you, too, Adam."

He smiled, the first smile she'd seen in a long while.

"We'll take care of each other, then," he said.

A few moments later they were heading down the
two-lane road back toward town. Barbed-wire fences

ran along both sides of the road with cows grazing in the green fields behind them. How ironic that such beauty and serenity could exist just a few feet from their car when her world seemed to be turning upside down.

Adam tensed beside her.

"What is it?" she asked.

"I remember where I saw that signature before, the name Judge Martin Jackson. That's the same judge who ruled on the case involving your adoptive father."

Her hands curled against the seat beside her. "You mean...the abuse case? My abuse case?"

He nodded. "I told you that my dad's a retired federal judge. From what I heard growing up, judges specialize and tend to stay in their specialties. It doesn't make sense to me that a family court judge is signing a bunch of real estate transaction documents. Even if he did switch specialties, the coincidence is sending up all kinds of red flags."

"What coincidence? The real estate transactions have nothing to do with me."

"They have everything to do with you. Your boss was looking into them and hid the evidence in your storage unit. Those have to be the documents Damien was talking about. He said pictures, and maybe there are some pictures, too. But maybe he meant documents, or whoever hired him didn't know if someone had physical printouts or just photographs." He waved his hand. "Doesn't matter. What does matter is that the same judge who signed them played a huge role in your life early on, signing other legal papers associated with you. Sam asked you about your birth parents. And your adoptive parents. Then he hid those papers where you'd eventually find them. Why would he do that if all of this isn't connected?"

He stared through the windshield at the winding road in front of them. His hands tightened on the steering wheel. "Didn't you tell me that Peter was a real estate developer? That he was always amassing property in the mountains?"

A cold chill seemed to run up her spine. "You think… you think he's somehow connected to all of this? Because the papers are about real estate?" She gave a humorless laugh. "That's quite a leap."

They drove in silence for a moment, then Adam slammed a hand against the steering wheel. "The timeline. That's it."

"What?"

"The timeline. Three days. You said Damien told you that Sam's PI firm had been a problem for three days. That was on Saturday. What happened three days before Saturday? What happened on Wednesday of last week?"

The truth slammed into her. She started to shake. "The councilman was murdered."

"Exactly. And he was helping a senator with the infrastructure bill. The government has to buy out everyone who owns land that they need for right of way. Which means researching titles and deeds and finding out who the owners are. That's what the councilman was helping with, because the land involved was here in Gatlinburg."

"Where my adoptive father owns a lot of real estate."

"Do *you*?"

She frowned. "What?"

"You told me your biological parents wanted to make sure you were taken care of. And yet their house passed to your adoptive family instead of to you. That seems unusual, to say the least. Isn't it also surprising that they didn't give you a generous enough trust fund to see you through life, not just college, but they left a huge fund for the Ingrams to take care of a house?"

She rubbed her arms again. "The thought has definitely crossed my mind before, yes."

"A judge ruled against you when you had the trust fund audited. Was that Judge Jackson, too?"

"No. I don't remember the judge's name, but it was a woman. It wasn't Martin Jackson."

"Then the audit may have been legit. Which again brings to question why your parents wouldn't provide better for you. The answer could be that they left you other investments, like real estate. They may have left you a fortune in land thinking it always appreciates in value and you'd be set for life, that you could sell some of it whenever you needed more money."

"But I didn't get *any* assets in the will other than the trust fund."

He tapped the folder on the seat between them. "You sure about that? Wills can be faked. Sam was tracing the titles on all of the land in this folder, either for a secret client that we haven't found yet or because he heard something himself that made him suspicious and decided to follow up. Either way, it leads back to you. Because he left the information in your storage unit, for you to find. Maybe the land in that folder was actually owned at one time by the Radcliffes—your biological parents. Which means the land should have passed to you but never did. Sam got sloppy, took one picture too many, and Damien or maybe Peter saw him. They went through his things, realized he'd figured out what they were doing—making a killing, probably millions of dollars—selling your land to the government as part of that infrastructure bill. They have to destroy any hint of impropriety about those land deals or they'll lose everything and wind up in prison."

She pressed a hand against her throat. "If you're right, my adoptive father wants me—"

"Dead. So he can enjoy the millions of dollars that were supposed to be yours." He tapped the folder again. "This is what he wants. Once he has it and any pictures that Sam hid, there's no reason to keep you alive any longer. You're a liability, a time bomb waiting to blow up his financial empire if you ever decide to contest the will and dig into your parents' financial history. As soon as we get this information to Duncan, we'll both grab a suitcase and head out of town to lie low somewhere until this is resolved. No arguments. I want you safe and as far away from Peter Ingram as possible."

"No arguments from me."

A black Dodge Charger came into view on the next hill up ahead, coming toward them.

Jody blinked and leaned forward in her seat. "Adam, that car. It looks just like the one that was parked near the Sugarland Mountain trailhead. The one Damien was driving."

Adam stared hard at the car coming their way. The

Charger sped past them with a familiar profile sitting in the driver's seat.

"Adam—"

"I know. It was Damien. Grab my phone. Call Duncan." He kept driving down the road, heading toward his house. When he glanced in the rearview mirror, he swore.

Jody whirled around in her seat. The Charger had hit the brakes. Damien was making a three-point turn in the middle of the road. The car took off, heading straight for them.

"My phone, Jody. Forget Duncan. Call 911."

She grabbed his cell phone out of his pants pocket, her breaths coming in ragged gasps. "What's your pass code?"

He told her, and she punched in the numbers.

Adam grabbed his pistol out of the holster and slammed the accelerator. His car was a sleek sedan with leather seats and all the creature comforts his money could buy. But it didn't have the horsepower the Charger had. Damien was rapidly gaining on them.

"We're four miles from my house. We aren't going to make it." He reached up and slammed back the inside cover of the moon roof.

"What are you doing?" Jody punched Send on the call.

"You're going to hold the wheel while I shoot the bastard. Did you call 911?"

"I did but nothing's happening!" She yanked the phone back to look at the screen. "The call didn't go through!" Her hands shook as she redialed.

Tat-tat-tat-tat-tat-tat-tat!
Bam! Bam!

The car bumped and swerved, skidding toward the drainage ditch on the side of the road.

Adam fought the wheel. "The tires! Hold on!"

"Nine-one-one, what's your emergency?" A tinny voice came through the phone.

She clung to the armrest as the car headed toward the ditch and a group of trees on the edge of the road. "This is Jody Ingram and Special Agent Adam McKenzie," she said so fast the words ran together. "Damien Flint's shooting at us on the road to Rutherford—"

"Brace yourself!" Adam yelled.

She screamed. The car slid off the road, hopped the ditch and slammed into a tree. Everything went black.

Chapter Twenty-Two

"You idiot! Bringing them here was the last thing you should have done. What if someone saw you?"

"No one saw me. I brought you the folder! After all the trouble I've gone through, including getting stabbed, you should be thanking me instead of yelling at me. My guys are hiding the car. No harm done."

A string of violent curses followed.

The words drifted through Jody's mind like a canoe slogging through mud. Someone was shouting at someone else. Both of the voices seemed to be coming through a long tunnel. They were achingly familiar. Not in a good way. She groaned and pressed a hand to her throbbing head.

"Jody?" Another voice, whispering next to her ear. Deep, soothing, full of concern.

"Adam?"

"Thank God." He pulled her close. "Where do you hurt?"

She blinked and opened her eyes. Then promptly closed them, her stomach lurching. "The room is spinning."

"You lost consciousness. You probably have a concussion. What about your arms? Your legs? I didn't see any cuts or obvious breaks. Does anything other than your head hurt?"

"Everything hurts."

"I know, sweetheart. I'm so sorry. Can you try to open your eyes again?"

More shouting. Something about deeds and pictures and…infrastructure? That voice. She knew that voice. It was…oh no!

Her eyes popped open. The room was still moving, but not as badly as before. She was sitting on the floor, her back against a wall. Adam knelt in front of her, the side of his head smeared with blood yet again.

He smiled. "There you are. Better now? The room isn't spinning?"

She reached out a shaky hand. "Your head. You're always getting hurt."

He ducked away. "I'm fine. Now that you're back in the land of the living, let's work on getting out of here. Do you know where we are?"

She looked past him and winced. "My room. My old room. When I was a little girl."

"One of Damien's men carried you up here. After Damien shot out our tires, we crashed. You hit your head on the side window." He framed her face in his hands and pressed a whisper-soft kiss against her lips. "You scared me to death. I thought I might lose you."

She clung to his hands. "What happened? Why are we here? Is that my…is Peter downstairs?"

He nodded again. "Damien had a submachine gun.

I lost my pistol in the crash and couldn't do anything to stop him."

She reached down to her side.

"Your gun is gone, too," he told her. "We don't have any weapons. But that doesn't mean we're defenseless. As long as they're arguing, we know where they are. Can you stand?" He didn't wait for her reply. He grabbed her around the waist and lifted her to her feet.

She'd squeezed her eyes shut because the room was spinning again. But when she realized she was clutching his shoulders to steady herself, and that she was bending over at the waist to do it, she forced her eyes open again. Adam was still kneeling on the floor.

"Good job," he said. "I've tied some bedsheets together and anchored them to the four-poster bed. You need to climb out that window and run. Looks like there are some trees ten yards out. That should give you good cover." He tugged her hand to get her moving.

She pulled her hand out of his grasp. "Where are your crutches? Did those monsters take them away from you? I'm not leaving you here."

He frowned. "Jody, we don't have time to argue. We don't know whether that 911 call did any good. You didn't have time to give them an address. We have to assume that help isn't coming."

"I told them Rutherford Estates. And we crashed. They'll see our car, look for us. They have our names. Why are you shaking your head?"

"You said Rutherford. And you gave them our names. They'll look me up and realize I live in Rutherford Estates, so they'll go to my house. Not here."

"But the car. Surely they'll see the crash, know something is wrong. When they don't find us at your house, won't they search the whole subdivision, go door to door? Canvassing. That's what it's called, right?"

"From what I could tell from the yelling downstairs, it sounds like Damien and his guys cleaned up the accident scene. I don't know that the police will have cause to go door to door searching for us." He frowned and glanced past her toward the door, which she noted no longer had the dead bolt on it that someone had installed for her years ago.

"I don't hear them anymore," he said. "You need to hurry. I'll do what I can to stall them. But you have to get out of here." He pushed her toward the window again.

She shoved his hand away. "You can't even stand. I'm not leaving you."

He grabbed one of the posts on the bed's footboard and shoved to his feet. "There. I'm standing. I'm not helpless. Now go."

"You're as white as a sheet."

"It hurts, all right? But I'm fine. Please, Jody. Just go."

Fresh blood marked the denim of his jeans. He wasn't even close to fine, and they both knew it. She took a quick look around. Everything in the room was eerily similar to the way it had looked when she was little, probably because the house was so large there was no reason to redecorate this particular room. Dust covers were draped over the bed, the chair in the corner, the desk. If all of her things were still here, there were crutches she'd used when her adoptive father had slammed her into a wall and broken her leg. They'd be too short. But maybe Adam could still use them like canes to help him walk, like he'd done with the tree branch in the mountains. She ran to the closet.

"Jody, what are you doing? Get out of here."

"I'm not leaving you. So quit telling me to go." She flipped the light on and rushed inside. Her stomach dropped when she saw nothing that looked familiar. The large closet was obviously being used for storage now. There were boxes stacked in neat rows all across the back. Labels declared them as "crafts." Probably for Amelia. She'd always loved making things and took up new craft hobbies all the time. Or at least she used to. There might be something in these boxes Jody could use.

She started tearing them open. In the third one, she found nylon rope used for macramé, along with a pair of scissors. In another box she found picture frames and a shadow box. She yanked out the shadow box and broke it apart. The pieces of wood were thick and long, perfect for making a splint. She'd have Adam fixed up in no time. Then both of them could climb out of the window together.

Holding the rope and wood in one hand, scissors in the other, she hurried back into the bedroom. Her mouth dropped open in horror, and she stumbled to a halt. Adam was still standing with one hand holding the bedpost. But he had a wicked-looking long gun pointed at him, and Damien was holding it.

"Well, well, well. The last little PI finally makes an

appearance." He nodded toward his left arm, still in a sling. "Maybe I'll get a chance for payback after all. Drop the scissors and that other junk." He jerked his head toward the open bedroom door. "Daddy's waiting."

She cast a miserable glance toward Adam and dropped her splint supplies to the floor. He was right. She should have gone out the window. Now there would be no help for him, or her. "I'm so sorry, Adam."

He gave her an encouraging smile without a hint of anger. "Go on. We'll be okay."

Damien laughed. "Sure, yeah, you'll be okay." He chuckled and jerked his head again. "After you."

Jody straightened her spine and headed into the hallway.

"Now you, *cop.* Go."

A loud thump sounded behind her, followed by a pained grunt.

Damien cursed.

Jody spun around.

Adam was on his hands and knees. He must have fallen. Damien pulled his leg back as if to kick him.

Jody ran forward. "Don't touch him!"

Damien turned the gun on her. "Back. Off." He aimed his gun at her abdomen.

"I'm okay. Jody, get out of here. Go." Adam hauled himself upright, using the bed for support again. "I'm okay."

She rushed to him in spite of his protests and the gun following her every move. She shoved her shoulder under his left arm, acting as his crutch.

He gave her an admonishing look, once again not

happy that she'd put herself in more danger to help him. But he didn't argue as he limped with her out of the room under the watchful gaze of Damien and his gun.

Going downstairs was much easier because he used the banister and hopped down each step. But once they were on the ground floor without a banister to hold, he had to lean on her in order to limp into the family room.

"Stop right there," Damien ordered.

They stopped in the middle of the room. Ned and another armed man they'd never seen before lounged against the left side of the massive fireplace. A third gunman stood on the right side of the fireplace. Damien crossed the room and joined him. And directly in the middle, ten feet away from her and Adam, stood the man who'd made her childhood worse than any nightmare.

His dark brown hair was stylishly short with just a hint of gray at the temples. The charcoal-colored suit he wore was tailored perfectly to compliment his broad shoulders and trim waist. Gold cuff links winked in the light of the chandelier suspended from the twenty-foot ceiling above them. To anyone else, he'd look like a handsome businessman, perfectly groomed and ready for an important meeting. To Jody, he looked like a monster.

She started to shake.

Adam's arm tightened around her shoulders.

A loud crash sounded off to their left. Everyone turned toward the sound, except the monster. He let out a deep sigh and simply turned his head to look at the woman who'd just emerged from the kitchen and had dropped a tray of drinks onto the travertine floor, shattering the glasses. She stared at Jody, her eyes big and round, her mouth dropping open.

"Amelia," the monster said. "Our daughter has finally come home to visit."

Her mother didn't move, didn't say anything. She just stared at Jody in obvious horror.

Footsteps sounded.

Jody looked toward her adoptive father. His polished shoes clicked against the floor as he strode toward her.

Adam tensed.

Peter stopped three feet away and sighed heavily again. "Jody, Jody, Jody. Always the troublemaker. Maybe I should take you upstairs and turn you over my knee, eh? Teach you another lesson?"

"You'll never touch a hair on her head again, you lecherous pervert," Adam snapped.

Peter's eyes narrowed.

A muffled sob sounded from Amelia. She whirled around and ran into the kitchen.

Peter rolled his eyes and shook his head. Ignoring Adam, he stared at Jody, a nauseatingly hungry look in his eyes. "If I only had more time." He clucked his tongue. "But I have a funeral to attend. A dear friend died tragically in a car crash last week." He chuckled again. "Seems to happen a lot to my friends. Car crashes." He winked.

Jody's stomach lurched at the implication. Her parents, her real ones, had died in a car crash. Had Peter had something to do with that too?

"Fortunately for me—" his voice was lowered in a

conspiratorial tone "—my dear friend had finished the task I gave him before his…demise."

"Forging land leases?" Adam accused. "Helping you arrange accidents for the true owners? Convincing Senator Sinclair to push an infrastructure bill so you could sell all the land you stole to the government and make a fortune?"

Peter slowly turned his head like a snake and speared Adam with his dark-eyed gaze. "To be fair, I bought some of that land legitimately."

"You didn't buy *Jody's* land legitimately. You stole her inheritance. Including this house."

"Well, well, well. Someone's been busy, haven't they? Faking that damn will cost me a pretty penny. I spent years covering that up. And all it took was one very stupid drunk councilman in a bar to complain to the wrong PI about the problems he was having performing title searches to bring it all crashing down around my ears. I gave him explicit instructions to exclude the Radcliffe properties from those searches. But he wasn't the detail-oriented man he should have been. And Sam Campbell started sticking his nose where it didn't belong. Who knew he'd recognize the Radcliffe name? My bad luck that you were working for him. Doesn't matter now, though."

"I'll bet you killed the councilman. And you killed Sam," Jody accused. "And Tracy. And my real parents. For what? Land? Money?" She waved her hand to encompass the mansion. "By all accounts you were quite wealthy even before my parents' deaths. And now you have this. Don't you have enough already?"

He smiled. "You poor, silly girl. You can never have enough when it comes to money."

She surged forward, wanting to slam her fists into his smiling face. But Adam tightened his arm around her shoulders, anchoring her against him. He turned his body slightly as if to protect her from her adoptive father. It caused her arm around his waist to bump against something beneath his shirt, something in his back pocket.

She glanced up at him. He was staring intently at her. *The scissors.*

That's what was in his pocket. He must have fallen on purpose in her bedroom so he could grab them. And he was letting her know he would use them when the time was right. But how could the time ever be right with four gunmen twenty feet away? And who knew if Peter was armed? She cleared her throat and looked back at the monster.

"You have the land and the folder," she said. "I don't have any proof that you stole anything from me. It would just be my word against yours. You can let us go."

He clucked his tongue again. "Right. And your boyfriend here would just ignore everything that's happened? He's a cop. Cops don't ignore and let things go. At least, not the honest ones who refuse to take bribes. And word on the street is that he's one of the good guys. Which means, of course, you both have to die."

"Bribes?" Adam said, obviously stalling for time. "Just like you bribed Judge Jackson when Jody went to court? And bribed him again to file those bogus land claims?"

Peter speared him with a look full of hate. "You know way too much, cop."

"What about the pictures?" Damien stepped forward. "I chased them through those stupid mountains to find out where that PI hid the pictures. There weren't any pictures in the folder."

Peter rolled his eyes, a pained expression on his face. "There were never any pictures, *you moron*. I made that up because you didn't need to know exactly what I was looking for. You were just supposed to find out where Campbell might hide any information he collected." He pointed at a folder lying on a decorative table against the wall. The folder that had been in Jody's storage unit. "Everything I need is in there. Now all you have to do is kill these two and I'll be on my way."

"No." The voice, barely above a whisper, came from the kitchen doorway.

Everyone turned to see Amelia once again standing there. This time she was holding a pistol. And it was pointed at her husband.

"Ho, ho," Damien exclaimed, laughing. "Trouble in paradise, boss?"

"Shut up." Peter stared at his wife. "What do you think you're doing, Amelia?"

"What I should have done when Jody was a little girl. Stopping you." Her lower lip wobbled and the gun shook in her hand. "I'm so sorry, Jody. I swear I never even suspected that he might be hurting you until that counselor from your school talked to me."

"Shut *up*, woman." Peter strode toward Amelia. "She lied. I never did *anything* to her."

Amelia wrapped both hands around the gun and brought it up higher, pointing directly at Peter's head. This time, her hands weren't shaking. "Not one step closer. I'll shoot you. I will."

He stopped, his eyes narrowing. "Now why would you do that?"

"Because you hurt little girls!" she cried out. She looked toward Jody. "I swear, I never knew. I asked Patricia and Patience when your counselor brought those charges against Peter. But they said you were lying, that their daddy would never do that. He would never do those horrible, awful things." Tears spilled over and slid down her cheeks. The gun started shaking again. "They were little girls, too. I believed them. I never knew they were scared of him, that they lied. For him. Until Patricia had her baby last month. And she and her husband wouldn't let Peter near the baby." A sob burst between her clenched teeth. "Oh, God. Your own daughters. How could you, Peter?"

His face turned a bright red. He looked at Damien. "Shoot her."

Damien's men raised their guns.

Adam took a limping step forward, his hand going behind his back. Jody grabbed his arm, but he shook it off.

"Adam," she whispered, "please don't. They'll kill you."

He took another wobbling step and pulled the scissors out of his waistband.

"Hold it," Damien said, raising his hand and motioning toward his men. "Lower your weapons."

Adam stopped, the scissors clutched in his right hand. But no one seemed to notice. They were all looking back and forth between Amelia, Peter and Damien.

Adam took another step, and another, moving closer to Peter, the scissors down by his side, half concealed by his hand.

Jody wanted to grab him, stop him. Instead, she moved with him, trying to keep from having a big gap between them to make it less obvious that he'd moved closer to Peter.

Damien faced his boss. "You some kind of perv, man? You like to hurt little girls?"

Peter looked down his nose at Damien. "You're a murderer and a thug. Don't tell me you're suddenly developing a conscience."

Sirens sounded in the distance.

Damien and his men exchanged worried glances.

"Don't be idiots," Peter said. "They're going somewhere else. Not here."

"Yeah, well. We ain't taking that chance," Damien replied. "Not for some sicko who hurts kids." He motioned to his men and they headed for the door.

Peter stepped toward them. "One million dollars. I'll give one million dollars to the man who shoots my wife."

Jody gasped.

Amelia's eyes widened.

All four men turned around.

"A million?" one of them asked, aiming his gun at Amelia.

"No." This time it was Adam who stepped forward.

The man turned his gun toward Adam.

Jody stepped forward. "No!"

Adam shoved her behind him. "You really want to go to jail for a pedophile?"

The man's gaze darted to Peter, who was now glaring at Adam.

"Even if you don't care what he's done," Adam continued, his voice calm, matter-of-fact, "do you think you can trust him to follow through with the money?"

"Two million!" Peter yelled.

The man swung his pistol back toward Amelia.

She stood frozen, tears tracking down her chin. She didn't seem to know what to do and was obviously too scared to pull the trigger on her gun to defend herself.

"Wait!" Adam yelled.

The man looked at him but kept his gun trained on Amelia.

"He's asking you to kill his wife," Adam said. "You really think he'll honor his word to you, someone he barely knows? Everything he does is about money and protecting himself. And you think he'll give you a million dollars, two million dollars? More likely he'll hire someone else to take you out for a few thousand. He kills everyone who gets in his way or threatens what he wants. Listen to the sirens. The police are almost here."

The sirens were much louder now. But were they coming here? Or to Adam's house a few blocks away?

Adam took another step forward. "When the police get here and find Amelia dead, what do you think Peter will tell them? That you killed her. A home invasion. He'll blame everything that happens here on you. The forensics will back him up. You go to prison. He goes on to enjoy his millions."

The gunmen shared concerned looks. One of them headed out the door. Ned followed, leaving Damien and the other gunman.

"Those cops aren't coming here," Damien said, looking like he was considering cashing in on Peter's offer.

"Of course they aren't," Peter said. "No one has any reason to suspect me of anything. You and your men made sure of it."

"Jody called 911," Adam rushed to say. "Right before the crash. They're definitely coming here. Sounds to me like they're three or four minutes out. You'd better hurry and decide whether you want to go to prison or get out of here."

"Check her phone," Damien ordered the other gunman. "Hurry."

"I don't have it," Jody started to say, thinking she'd lost Adam's phone in the crash. But the gunman pulled the phone out of his own pocket.

"Pass code," Damien said. "What's the code to unlock it?"

She gave him the code that Adam had given her in the car. The gunman keyed it in and swiped the screen a few times. His face went pale. "She ain't lying. She called 911."

"Screw it," Damien said. "Let's get out of here. Wait in the Charger. I'll be right there."

His partner threw the phone down and ran out the door.

"Did he really hurt you as a little girl?" Damien asked, looking straight at Jody.

Her face flushed with heat. "Yes."

"Sick bastard." Damien pointed his gun at Peter.

Peter threw his hands up. "My lawyer is working to get your brother out of jail. You kill me and what do you think he'll do?"

"Come on, man!" A yell came from outside.

Damien's hand flexed on the gun. "You'd better not renege on our deal or I'll come after you, you sicko." He tossed his gun toward Peter and ran.

Peter caught the gun and swung it toward Amelia.

"No!" Adam threw the scissors like a javelin toward Peter.

Boom! Boom!

Peter fell to the floor, the scissors embedded deep in his neck. He gagged and clasped his hands around the wound, blood pouring through the gaps between his fingers. His knees drew up, blood darkening his pants where Amelia's bullet had found its mark.

He'd never hurt another little girl again.

Jody whirled around toward Amelia. "Oh no! Mom!"

Amelia blinked in confusion and looked down. Red bloomed on her breast above her heart and quickly spread, saturating her shirt. Peter's bullet had found its mark, too.

Jody ran to her, catching her just as Amelia's knees buckled beneath her. She couldn't hold her up and fell with her to the floor.

"Mom, Mom. Oh no, please. Mom." She pressed her hands against the wound, desperately trying to stop the bleeding.

Adam dropped to the floor beside her, his phone in

his hand. "We need an ambulance." He rattled off the address that he'd found on the internet just last night while looking into Jody's past. "Send the police, too," he said. "I hear them in the subdivision. They're probably at my home from a previous 911 call, but we're here. We're the ones who called them."

"Jody?" Amelia blinked up at her. "Are you there?"

Tears flooded Jody's eyes. "Yes. I'm here."

Adam yanked off his shirt and pushed Jody's hands away. "I've got it." He pressed his shirt hard against the wound.

Amelia gasped, her lips turning white.

"Sorry, Mrs. Ingram. I have to press hard to stop the bleeding."

Jody grabbed Amelia's hand and held it tightly in her own as she gently wiped the hair out of Amelia's face. "Hold on. Help is on the way."

Amelia blinked, and her vision seemed to clear, her hand tightening on Jody's. "Sweet, sweet girl. I'm so sorry. I swear, I never knew. I didn't."

"It's okay," Jody whispered, her tears dropping onto their joined hands. "It's okay."

"No. It's not." Amelia coughed, and bright red blood bubbled out of her mouth.

"Don't try to talk." Jody gently wiped the blood away. "Save your strength."

"I put the lock on your door." Amelia clung to Jody's hand and searched her gaze. "I didn't think you were telling the truth. But I put the lock on your door to be sure, as a test. He never…he never said anything, never took it off. So I thought… I thought that proved me right. That he wasn't the man you said he was." She coughed again and started choking.

"Jody, back up."

She scooted back and Adam rolled Amelia onto her side. She stopped coughing. He moved forward, his knees propping her up while he applied pressure to her wound again.

Jody bent down, maintaining eye contact. Amelia was frighteningly pale, her eyes turning glassy.

"Jody?"

"I'm here." Her voice broke as she clasped Amelia's hands. "I won't leave you. I'm here."

"I loved you, Jody. I should have been stronger, smarter. I should have fought for you."

"You did. He never hurt me again after you put that lock on my door," Jody said, her heart breaking. "I love you, too. You were the only mother I ever knew. It's okay. Everything is going to be okay."

"Forgive me?" Amelia pleaded. "Please forgive me."

"I forgive you."

A smile curved her mother's red-stained lips. Then her hand went slack in Jody's.

"Mama?" She shook Amelia's hand. "Mama?"

"Miss, let us help her," a voice said behind her.

"Mama?"

Adam was suddenly there, pulling her back. "Let her go, Jody. You have to let her go."

"No! Mama?"

Adam lifted her in his arms, then limped to one of the couches and collapsed onto the cushions, holding her tightly against him.

"Shh," he whispered against the top of her head. "Shh."

He stroked her back and rocked her as the paramedics worked on Amelia. Jody drew a ragged breath and closed her eyes, clinging to him and doing something she hadn't done since she was a little girl and a judge sent her back to live with the monster.

She prayed.

Chapter Twenty-Three

Three months later, Jody stood at the entrance to the Sugarland Mountain Trail, a jacket around her to ward off the chilly autumn temps up high in the mountains. A backpack of supplies was strapped on her shoulders. Sensible boots protected her feet, gave her sure footing.

There was no cattle gate across the entrance this time, no warning signs declaring that the trail was closed, no man with a gun chasing her. She was all alone and ready to begin another journey, another chapter of her life.

She pulled her cell phone out of her pants pocket. No bars, no service. But it showed the time. She'd been checking it every few minutes. When she realized the wait was over, a mixture of dread and excitement sent a shot of adrenaline through her. This was it. No turning back now. She started up the path.

Her steps were measured, careful. She kept glancing at her phone, checking the time, checking her surroundings to get her bearings. She didn't want to be late. Or early. She wanted everything to be perfect.

A few minutes later, she reached the curve in the

path, the one where Adam had disappeared all those months ago as he chased Damien. The one where she and Adam had run back the other way with two gunmen after them.

Her pulse sped up, her body shaking. She pushed back the fear, knowing it was silly now. Damien and his men weren't chasing her this time. The police had rounded up everyone involved in Peter Ingram's schemes, and they were all either already convicted and in prison or in jail waiting for their trials. She was safe. No reason to be afraid.

Well, at least not about bad guys, anyway.

She forced her feet forward and rounded the curve, then hurried to her destination. When she reached the spot where Adam had forced her to take that huge leap of faith, she stopped. And looked out at the mountains and the Chimney Tops beyond. And waited.

"Jody?"

His voice sent a jolt of yearning straight through her. She drew a deep breath and turned.

Adam stood ten feet away, having just come around the corner from the other direction. He was wearing his ranger's uniform again, his gun holstered at his side, his new radio clipped to his belt.

"How's the leg?" She waved toward his left leg, which had a metal brace around it from ankle to knee.

He took a step toward her, then stopped again, his gaze wary. "It's fine. Thanks."

She swallowed, hating that she'd been the reason for that wariness. "This is your first day back on the job, isn't it?"

He frowned. "How did you know?"

She took a step toward him. "I asked your brother. Duncan."

His jaw tightened. "He told you I was walking this trail, didn't he?"

She nodded.

"Why? Why are you here?"

She took another step forward. "You're not going to make this easy, are you?"

He looked away, out toward the Chimney Tops. "I don't know what you want from me, Jody. I tried visiting, calling, texting, emailing, until I felt like a stalker and had to stop." He looked back at her. "It's been three months since your…since Peter Ingram died. You haven't contacted me once."

She moved closer. "I know. I'm sorry. I'm so sorry."

"You say that all the time. It doesn't mean anything anymore."

She sighed and raked her hair back. "You're right. I'm trying to stop apologizing so much. I've been going to therapy again, trying to move on, letting go of all the guilt I've been carrying around." She let out a harsh laugh. "At least I've finally figured out why I've always felt so guilty."

"Your sisters. You blame yourself for leaving when you turned eighteen. You've worried that you didn't fight for them, too. You left them behind, and it's always bothered you."

She blinked. "How do you know that?"

He gave her a sad smile. "Because I know *you*, Jody Vanessa Radcliffe."

She blinked again. "How did you know I changed my last name?"

He tapped the badge clipped to his belt. "Cop." He dropped his hand to his side. "Or I might have heard it from Duncan. He told me he'd offered you an investigator job with the National Park Service. You had to put your legal name on the paperwork."

She smiled. "You've been keeping tabs on me."

"Not since the first month. Like I said, I felt like a stalker, so I quit. Duncan, on the other hand, won't stop talking about you. He's torturing me." He clamped his lips together and looked away.

"Torturing you?" She took another step. "Hearing about me is torture?"

His fingers curled into his palms, but he didn't say anything.

"It's been torture for me, too," she admitted. "Being away from you."

His gaze shot to hers. Still, he said nothing.

"My mom's fine, in case you're wondering. You saved her life that day. You kept your cool, thought to grab the phone and call for help when I was completely losing it. The doctors said if you hadn't gotten the EMTs there so fast, if you hadn't kept pressure on the wound, she'd be dead. Thank you, Adam. Thank you for saving her."

He shook his head. "I did my job. And we were lucky you'd called 911 and the police and EMTs were already at my house."

"Maybe. Maybe not. You have a talent for saving

people." She took another step forward. "You saved me. So many times. In so many ways."

He stared at her, some of the hostility and frustration easing from his expression. The wariness was back. But along with it was something else. Hope.

"I needed the time, the distance," she said. "From you, from my overwhelming feelings for you. Because I didn't believe it could be real. We'd known each other for, what, a few days? Less than a week? Under traumatic circumstances. I didn't trust my feelings. I had to process them. And I had to process my 'unhealthy attitude' toward sex." She used air quotes. "Apparently my adoptive father did a number on my psyche and I never understood what a normal physical relationship was supposed to be like. Until you."

"You're giving me too much credit."

She shrugged. "Not in my opinion. But I'm working through my relationship hang-ups. And my relationships with my adoptive family. I had to deal with my mother in the hospital, her recovery, getting to know my sisters and brothers, unraveling the legal tangle that Peter Ingram left for all of us." She shook her head. "It was a mess. I was a mess. That's why I've been going to a therapist."

He started to step forward, then stopped. "Are you okay?" He cleared his throat. "I mean, your adoptive family, the legal stuff."

"My adoptive…my *family* is…well, awkward might be the best way to put it. My sisters weren't abused in spite of Amelia's fears, by the way. Thank God for that. But they suspected what their father had done to me.

That's why Patricia wouldn't let him be alone with her new daughter. She didn't trust him. Still, they grew up with him as their dad, loving him as best they could with all that poison running just beneath the surface. I think they blame me for what's happened to the family now. I can understand that. But I don't apologize to anyone for it. Like I said, I'm moving on. From the guilt, from my past." She stepped closer. "I'm moving toward my future now."

He looked down at her feet and smiled. "You're wearing boots."

"And a shiny new backpack with supplies. I learned my lesson from the best. Always be prepared for the worst." She took another step. "But hope for the best."

He stared at her intently, longingly, and took a step toward her. "I saw that your family house is for sale."

She nodded. "The courts awarded me all of the money, the house, even the land that Peter tried to swindle from me. The infrastructure deal is still going through. I didn't try to stop it. But all the money from the land sales went to me."

"You're rich now."

"In some people's eyes, maybe. I gave a huge chunk of it to my mother and siblings. Including the house. But no one wants to live there because of everything that happened. It was their decision to sell."

"You gave a multimillion-dollar mansion plus more money on top of that to your family? After they turned their backs on you? And didn't protect you?" His tone wasn't accusing, just curious and concerned. As always, it was her he was worried about. Which reassured her that this little trip into the mountains had been the right thing to do. She hadn't built him up in her mind as larger-than-life after all. He really was the wonderful, caring, protective man that she remembered from that dark time in her life that seemed so long ago now.

"I don't blame my adoptive family," she explained. "Not anymore. In their own way, they were all just as much victims as I was. If I kept all that money, it would make me feel like the villain of their lives. There's been too much hurt, too much hate in my life already. I didn't want that. I did it for me, more than for them. I also gave some to Tracy's family. They were there for me, always. So, for once, I was there for them. I'm here for you, now, Adam. If you still want me, that is."

"If I still want you?" He gave her an incredulous look. "Is that a joke?"

"I hope not."

He quickly closed the remaining distance between them. He pulled her into his arms and looked down at her, a fierce, hungry expression on his face. "I'll never stop wanting you. I want to kiss you. If you don't want that, you'd better tell me right now."

She wrapped her arms around his neck. "It's about time."

He groaned and claimed her mouth with his. It wasn't sweet or gentle like he'd been the first time he'd kissed her, when he'd shown her how a man who really cared about a woman treated her. This kiss was out of control, full of longing, yearning, and wild with desire. He was consuming her, and she was bursting into flames in his arms.

His tongue tangled with hers, and his hands roamed over her body, stroking, teasing, tempting. When he finally broke the kiss, they were both panting.

She stared up into his gorgeous blue eyes, gazing down at her with such yearning it nearly broke her heart. "I'm so sorry that I took so long to—"

"No apologizing." His voice was ragged, strained. He kissed her forehead and dragged her against him, his arms holding her tight. "I thought it was all in my head, that I was the only one who felt this way."

She pulled back so she could look up into his eyes, needing to hear the words. "Felt what way?"

He frowned, looking uncertain again. "I love you, Jody. Don't you know that?"

She burst into tears.

He lifted her in his arms. He carried her to one of the leftover stumps that still needed to be cleared from the trail and sat down with her in his lap. He rocked her and stroked her back. "Good tears?"

She hugged him tight. "Good tears. I'm trying not to cry so much. But it's going to take some work to change."

He set her back from him and cupped her face in his hands. "Don't change for me, Jody. Don't ever change. I love you just the way you are. Tears and all."

She hiccupped, and they both laughed.

"I love you, too, Adam. I think I loved you from the moment you threw me off that stupid cliff and sacrificed your own body to protect mine."

"I didn't throw you. I pulled you with me."

She rolled her eyes. "Just don't ever do it again. You scared me to death."

He kissed her, gently, softly, a fluttering caress like soft butterfly wings brushing against her heart. Then he smiled down at her with such reverence and love in his deep blue eyes that her tears started up again.

"I love you, Jody. I may not know everything about you. But I know what matters—your caring heart, your courageous, selfless soul, your kind and giving spirit. And I want to spend the rest of my life getting to know all of the fascinating details that go along with that. I want to build a future with you. If you'll have me."

She straightened in his arms. "What are you saying, Adam?"

His hands shook as he gently feathered her hair back from her face. "I'm saying that I want to marry you. But I know we've only really known each other a short time. I don't count the three months we've been apart. So I'll start out slow. We can date for a while. I'll introduce you to my family—my other brothers, Ian, too, if I can even locate him and convince him to come home for a visit. My mom, my dad. They have a cabin in the mountains where we grew up, where I got my love for the outdoors. I want to take you to Memphis, too. That's where I started my career, as a beat cop, before the ranger position opened up and I could come back here, to my hometown. I want to share everything with you. And then, when you're ready, once you feel you know me well enough, if you still think you love me, maybe then we can work on forever."

She shook her head in wonder. "You're an amazing

man, Adam McKenzie. And far more patient than me."
She shoved her hand into her jacket pocket and pulled
out a small velvet box and held it out to him. "Open it."

He frowned. "What are you doing?"

"What do you think I'm doing? I'm asking you to
marry me. There's a gold band in that box. I know it's
not the customary thing for a guy to wear an engage-
ment ring. But you're blazing hot and I want every
woman who looks at you to know you're taken."

"No."

She grew still in his arms. "No? You don't want to
marry me? But… I thought—"

He pressed a finger to her lips. "Hold that thought."
He reached behind him and unsnapped one of the small
leather holders clipped to his belt. Then he held his hand
out toward her. A large diamond sparkled in the sun-
light, surrounded by a smaller cluster of diamonds on
a white-gold band.

Tears flowed again, and she didn't even bother to
wipe them away. There was no point. She seemed to
have an endless supply. Her chin wobbled as she held
out her left hand.

He slid the ring onto her finger, then handed her the
gold band she'd gotten him. She put it on his finger and
stared up at him in wonder.

"When? When did you get that ring?" she asked.

"Right after the whole debacle at your old house.
Every time one of those thugs pointed a gun your way,
I felt like I was dying inside. I knew I was in love with
you and there was no point in fighting it. I've carried
that ring with me ever since, all the while hoping and

praying you'd come back to me. If, or when, you were ever ready."

He lifted her off his lap and set her on the stump, then got down on his one good knee.

"Jody Vanessa Radcliffe, will you make me the happiest man alive and agree to be my wife?"

"Only if you'll agree to make me the happiest woman in the world by being my husband."

He grinned. "I'll do my best."

"You always do, Adam. You always do."

He took her in his arms, and into his heart, and once again, he saved her.

* * * * *

Look for the next book in award-winning author Lena Diaz's The Mighty McKenzies miniseries, Smokies Special Agent, *available next month!*

COMING NEXT MONTH FROM

H HARLEQUIN®

INTRIGUE

Available April 16, 2019

#1851 SHOW OF FORCE
Declan's Defenders • by Elle James
When Russian spy Riley Lansing's handler kidnaps her younger brother to force her to assassinate someone, former marine Mack Balkman is the only one who can help her. Can they find the boy before time runs out?

#1852 SMOKIES SPECIAL AGENT
The Mighty McKenzies • by Lena Diaz
Ten years ago, FBI agent Remi Jordan's twin sister disappeared in the mountains. When Remi offers herself as bait to catch the killer, she finds herself at odds with Duncan McKenzie, the criminal investigator who is trying to keep her safe.

#1853 SNOWBOUND SUSPICION
Eagle Mountain Murder Mystery: Winter Storm Wedding
by Cindi Myers
Trapped by a snowstorm, caterer Bette Fuller knows US marshal Cody Rankin is the only man who can protect her from the Ice Cold Killer, a sadistic serial killer who is stalking her.

#1854 WYOMING COWBOY SNIPER
Carsons & Delaneys: Battle Tested • by Nicole Helm
Bad girl Vanessa Carson and uptight Dylan Delaney's drunken one-night stand has permanent consequences. It can't get worse...until they're kidnapped and Vanessa loses her memory.

#1855 CRIMINAL BEHAVIOR
Twilight's Children • by Amanda Stevens
Special Agent Ethan Barrow refuses to believe his father is a murderer. The only person who can help him prove his father's innocence is Detective Adaline Kinsella, the daughter of his father's alleged victim. Is the killer in jail...or is he stalking the people who are digging into the past?

#1856 K-9 DEFENSE
by Elizabeth Heiter
After former marine Colter Hayes and his combat tracker dog find Kensie Morgan in the Alaskan wilderness, Kensie is determined to enlist the pair's help in tracking down her little sister, who went missing fourteen years ago.

YOU CAN FIND MORE INFORMATION ON UPCOMING HARLEQUIN® TITLES, FREE EXCERPTS AND MORE AT WWW.HARLEQUIN.COM.

HICNM0419

Chapter One

Located at the end of a dead-end street, the derelict Victorian seemed to wither in the heat, the turrets and dormers sagging from time, neglect and decades of inclement weather. The gardens were lost, the maze of brick pathways broken and forgotten. The whole place wore an air of despair and long-buried secrets.

Those secrets and the steamy humidity stole Detective Adaline Kinsella's breath as she ducked under the crime-scene tape and pushed open the front door. It swung inward with an inevitable squeak, drawing a shiver.

She had the strangest sensation of déjà vu as she entered the house, and the experience both puzzled and unsettled her. She'd never been here before. Couldn't remember ever having driven down this street. But a nerve had been touched. Old memories had been triggered. If she listened closely enough, she could hear the echo of long-dead screams, but she knew that sound came straight from her nightmares.

She was just tired, Addie told herself. Five days of hiking, swimming and kayaking in ninety degree weather had taken a toll, and now she needed a vacation from her vacation.

For nearly a week, she'd remained sequestered in her aunt's lake house without access to cable or the internet. One day had spun into another, and for the better part of the week, Addie had thought she'd found heaven on earth in the Blue Ridge Mountains. But by Thursday she'd become restless to the point of pacing on the front porch. On Friday she'd awakened early, packed up her car and headed back to Charleston, arriving just after lunch to explosive headlines and the police department abuzz with a gruesome discovery.

The details of that find swirled in her head as she hovered in the foyer. The previous owner of the house, a recluse named Delmar Gainey, had died five years earlier in a nursing home, and the property had remained vacant until an enterprising house flipper had bought it at auction. The demo crew had noticed a fusty odor, but no one had sounded an alarm. It was the smell of old death, after all. The lingering aroma of disintegrating vermin and rotting vegetation. The house had flooded at least once, allowing in the deadly invasion of mold and mildew. The structure was a public health hazard that needed to be razed, but the flipper had been adamant about renovation—until his workers had uncovered human remains behind the living room walls.

Skeletal remains had also been found behind the dining room walls and beneath the rotting floorboards in the hallway. Seven bodies hidden away inside the abandoned house and seven more buried in the backyard. Fourteen victims so far, and the search had now been extended onto the adjacent property.

"Hello?" Addie called as she moved across the foyer to the rickety staircase. The house was oppressive and sweltering. No power meant no lights and no AC. Sweat trickled down her backbone and moistened her armpits. Furtive claws scratched overhead, and the sound deepened Addie's dread. Ever since she'd heard about the Gainey house, images had bombarded her. Now she pictured the ceiling collapsing and rat bodies dropping down on her. She had a thing about rats. Spiders and snakes she could handle, but rats…

Grimacing in disgust, she moved toward the archway on her right, peeking into the shadowy space she thought might once have been the dining room. The long windows were boarded up, allowing only thin slivers of light to creep in. She could smell dust from the demolished plaster and a whiff of putrefaction. Or was that, too, her imagination? Delmar Gainey's victims had been entombed in the walls for over two decades. Surely the scent would have disintegrated by now.

A memory flitted and was gone. The nightmares still tugged…

Addie suppressed another shiver and wondered why she had come.

Don't miss
Criminal Behavior *by Amanda Stevens,*
available May 2019 wherever
Harlequin® Intrigue *books and ebooks are sold.*

www.Harlequin.com

"You know, that look you're giving me feels like a truth serum," she said. "You really don't want me to start spilling all, do you?"

Judd stayed quiet, maybe considering her question. Considering, too, that her spilling might involve talking about this heat that was still between them. Heat that sizzled when her eyes cleared enough to actually see him.

He looked away from her.

Obviously, he wasn't in a spilling or hearing a spilling kind of mood. Too bad, because a quick discussion of sizzle, followed by some flirting, might have washed away her dark film of thoughts.

"How are you?" Cleo asked, but what she really wanted to know was why he'd felt the need to call his sponsor.

His mouth tightened enough to let her know he didn't want to discuss it, but it did get his gaze back on her. A long, lingering, smoldering gaze. Though Cleo had to admit that the smoldering part might be her own overly active imagination.

Or not.

Judd said a single word of really bad profanity, grabbed her shoulders and dragged her to him. His mouth was on hers before

Cleo could even make a sound. It turned out, though, that no sound was necessary because she got a full, head-on slam of the heat. And this time it wasn't just simmering around them. It rolled through her from head to toe.

Now she made a sound, one of pleasure, and the years vanished. It was as if they'd picked up where they'd left off seventeen years ago, when he'd been scorching her like this in his bed.

His taste. Yes. That was the same. Maybe with a manlier edge to it, but it was unmistakably Judd. Unmistakably incredible.

Cleo felt herself moving right into the kiss. Right into Judd, too. Unfortunately, the gearshift was in the way, but she still managed some more body-to-body contact when she slid against him and into his arms.

Judd deepened the kiss, and she let him. In fact, Cleo was reasonably sure that she would have let him do pretty much anything. Yep, he'd heated her up just that much.

Apparently, though, he hadn't made himself as mindless and needy as he had her, because he pulled back, cursed again and resumed his cop's stare. Though she did think his eyes were a little blurry.

They sat there, gazes connected, breaths gusting. Waiting. Since Cleo figured her gusty breaths weren't enough to allow her to speak, she just waited for Judd to say something memorable.

"Damn," he growled.

Okay, so maybe not memorable in the way she'd wanted. Definitely not romantic. But it was such a *Judd* reaction that it made her smile. Then laugh.

She leaned in, nipped his bottom lip with her teeth. "Don't worry, Judd. I'll be gentle with you."

Don't miss
Hot Texas Sunrise *by Delores Fossen,*
available April 2019 wherever
HQN Books and ebooks are sold.

www.HQNBooks.com